D0253346

A Ghostly Sight

I looked and spotted the old Ayers place halfway down the next block. It was handsome and dignified rising up in the center of the tree-lined street. Light poured out of every window downstairs, showing off the architectural details of the imposing facade. Cars were parked in almost every available spot along the curb, and people in Mardi Gras–style finery were laughing and chatting and hurrying toward the mansion. Even with the car windows shut, we could hear the lively jazz music drifting out into the night.

"Looks like you might be out of luck tonight, George," Ned said as we reached the house. "With all the lights and activity, the ghost will probably be hiding under the bed all night."

For once George didn't seem to have a retort. I glanced back and saw her staring out the side window. Her face had suddenly gone white beneath the blush and lipstick Bess had so carefully applied.

"What's wrong?" I asked.

"That!" George gasped, pointing out the window with a trembling finger.

NANCY DREW
girl detective®

Available from Aladdin Paperbacks

Keene, Carolyn.
Mardi Gras masquerade /
2008.
33305236871582
ca   01/30/17

NANCY DREW

DREW
girl detective ®

#28

Mardi Gras Masquerade

CAROLYN KEENE

Aladdin Paperbacks
New York   London   Toronto   Sydney

If you purchased this book without a cover, you should be aware that this book is stolen property. It was reported as "unsold and destroyed" to the publisher, and neither the author nor the publisher has received any payment for this "stripped book."

This book is a work of fiction. Any references to historical events, real people, or real locales are used fictitiously. Other names, characters, places, and incidents are the product of the author's imagination, and any resemblance to actual events or locales or persons, living or dead, is entirely coincidental.

❧ALADDIN PAPERBACKS
An imprint of Simon & Schuster Children's Publishing Division
1230 Avenue of the Americas, New York, NY 10020
Copyright © 2008 by Simon & Schuster, Inc.
All rights reserved, including the right of
reproduction in whole or in part in any form.
NANCY DREW, NANCY DREW: GIRL DETECTIVE, ALADDIN PAPER-
BACKS, and related logo are registered trademarks of Simon & Schuster, Inc.
Manufactured in the United States of America
First Aladdin Paperbacks edition February 2008
10 9 8 7
Library of Congress Control Number 2007924840
ISBN-13: 978-1-4169-5103-2
ISBN-10: 1-4169-5103-2
0312 OFF

Contents

Party Spirits

O w!" I shrieked. "You're killing me!"

"Chill out, Nancy." My friend Bess Marvin tugged at the zipper on the back of my dress. "Now, hold your breath."

I sucked in my stomach. Bess gave one last yank, and the zipper slid up without pinching any more skin.

Exhaling in a sigh of relief, I turned toward the full-length mirror in the corner of my bedroom. "Okay," I said, surveying my reflection. "That was worth it. This dress is totally amazing."

Bess came over and stood beside me. "We could both pass for Mardi Gras queens," she said with a smile.

I nodded, still staring at my gown. It was gorgeous—

the bodice was mostly green satin, but a strip of multi-colored harlequin-style fabric ran down the middle, extending all the way to the bottom of the full skirt. When we'd picked it out at the local costume shop, Bess had insisted that green would be perfect with my strawberry-blond hair and blue eyes. Looking at it now, I had to admit she was right.

My eyes slid over to Bess's reflection. With her peaches-and-cream complexion, curvy figure, and flair for fashion, she always looked good. But now she was absolutely stunning in an old-fashioned blue-and-gold gown made of satin, brocade, and lace. Velvet gloves covered her arms up to the elbows, and her blond hair was swept up into an elaborate style topped off with feathers and glittering beads.

Bess's cousin, George Fayne, glanced up at us. She had spent the last few minutes lounging on my bed, whistling "When the Saints Go Marching In" and fiddling with the buttons on her fancy new digital camera.

"Enough with the primping already," she said, rolling over onto her stomach. The skirt of her jester-style costume was hiked up over her knees, and her matching mask was perched atop her short, dark hair like a pair of sunglasses. "How long does it take you two to get dressed, anyway?"

"Hey, watch your skirt," Bess told her. "The costume

shop isn't going to be happy if you bring it back with the half the beads missing."

"Whatever." George sat up and swung her legs over the edge of the bed, making the bells on her ends of her curly-toed shoes tinkle. "I just want to get this show on the road. When's Ned getting here?"

I checked my watch. Unlike me, my boyfriend Ned Nickerson is almost always right on time. "Five minutes," I said.

"Sounds like someone's anxious to go out and show all of River Heights that she actually does know how to put on a dress," Bess teased her cousin.

I giggled as George rolled her eyes. She's the world's biggest tomboy. I could probably count on one hand the number of times I've seen her in a skirt of any kind, and I've known her for most of my life. Jeans and sneakers are much more her style.

"No way," I told Bess. "George doesn't want anyone to know it's her. That's why she's wearing a mask."

"Very funny." George held up her camera as Bess snorted with laughter. "You know why I'm going to the party. Everyone in town says the old Ayers place is haunted. You guys won't be laughing when I use this baby to prove it."

"Since when do you believe in ghosts?" I asked. George might be unrealistic and impractical about some things—like how much money she can *really* afford to spend at the camera store, for instance—but she doesn't usually believe in anything supernatural.

She shrugged. "I usually don't," she admitted. "But if I can get something weird on camera tonight and sell it to a TV show, that should pay back the cost of my new digital and then some!" She snapped a picture of me and Bess.

"Well, I'm glad you're coming tonight, no matter how silly the reason," I told her, leaning toward the mirror over my dresser to dab on some lip gloss. "I just hope this fund-raiser is successful. Poor old Mr. Ayers has been having a lot of trouble keeping up his house lately."

Jackson Ayers was the owner of a gorgeous old Georgian mansion over on West Union Street. The place had been in his family for generations, and it was easier to imagine George in a ballerina's tutu than it was to imagine Jackson living anywhere else. However, it was no secret that he'd been having trouble keeping up the place. Jackson had inherited a nice nest egg along with the house. He'd also had a long, successful career at Rackham Industries, the local tech conglomerate. But in the years since his retirement, he's had to deal with several major home repairs, rising property taxes, and bad investments. All that has whittled his fortune down to nearly nothing.

Luckily River Heights has a small but active historical society. The society wanted to help by raising money for improvements so Jackson could apply to list the mansion with the Antique Homes Registry. That way the place would be preserved even after he was gone. An Ayers family connection to New Orleans had inspired the idea of a Mardi Gras–style masquerade ball. And if what I'd heard was true, at least half the town had bought tickets for tonight's big event.

"I hope the ball raises lots of money too." Bess twirled in front of the mirror, smiling as her skirt flared out. "I'm just glad we get to donate to a worthy cause *and* dance the night away at the same time!"

"Girls! Your chauffeur's here!" Hannah Gruen's voice floated up the stairs. Hannah has been an important part of my family ever since my mother died when I was three. Her official job description is "housekeeper," but she's more like a family member to Dad and me. I can't imagine what we'd do without her.

"Don't forget your mask," Bess reminded me as I headed for the door.

"Oops." I scurried back and grabbed it off the desk. Unlike George's, which was held on by a piece of elastic like a Halloween mask, mine was perched on a glitter-encrusted stick. I held it up and peered at my friends through the eye holes, feeling very glamorous. "Ready to go?"

Soon all three of us were climbing into Ned's car. I held up my skirt to keep it from touching the wet ground. It had rained all morning and there were puddles everywhere.

Ned reached over to give my hand a squeeze as I climbed into the front seat beside him. "You look gorgeous," he told me.

"Thanks." I took in his outfit. He was wearing a dark suit with a harlequin vest that matched my dress. His brown hair was slicked back, and a black mask decorated with swirls of gold, green, and purple glitter lay on the dashboard. "You don't look too shabby yourself."

"Watch my skirt!" Bess exclaimed, scooting across the backseat as George flopped down beside her. She gave George a shove.

"Hey! Watch the Nikon!" George yanked her camera out of harm's way.

"George is planning to do a little ghost busting tonight," I told Ned.

"Looking for the Ayers ghost, huh, George?" Ned smiled. "The *Bugle* did a little human-interest piece on that last Halloween." Ned's father is editor of the local newspaper, and Ned works there part-time.

"Uh-huh. I saw that article when I did some more

research on the Internet last night." George's voice took on the eager tone that she usually reserved for talk of her latest electronic or computer gadget. "It's a pretty cool story. Around the turn of the last century, this guy Maxwell Ayers—that's Jackson Ayers's grandfather, I think—moved to New Orleans after college. While he was there, he met this beautiful young woman named Lisette."

"Ooh, that's a pretty name," Bess put in.

George nodded, looking a bit impatient. "Anyway, the two of them fell in love and blah, blah, blah."

"You're such a romantic, George," Ned said, sounding amused.

George ignored him. "Lisette was from kind of an important New Orleans family. They lived there for generations and were very wealthy and all," she continued, leaning back against the car door. "Her mother was once the queen of the Mardi Gras parade, which I guess is a pretty big deal down there. And everyone thought Lisette was destined for the same thing, since she was so beautiful and charming and all that."

"Is that what happened? Did Lisette become a Mardi Gras queen?" I asked, glancing over my shoulder at my friends in the backseat.

George shook her head. "Not exactly. See, she and Maxwell Ayers were totally planning to get married, stay in New Orleans, and create a life there together.

But then Maxwell's father died suddenly, which left his mother and a bunch of younger siblings with nobody to support them." She shrugged. "So they called Maxwell to come back to River Heights and take care of them."

"Sad," Ned commented as he turned onto Bluff Street. "Kind of a bummer for Maxwell, too."

"Totally," George agreed. "But what could he do? He had to go. He talked Lisette into coming north with him, promising her that one day soon, when the family was financially secure again, the two of them would go back to New Orleans. She was in love, so she agreed, even though she'd never been more than like ten miles from New Orleans in her whole life. They came up here and moved into the family mansion."

"The one where Jackson Ayers lives now?" Ned asked.

George nodded. "The same one we're going to tonight," she said. "Maxwell went into the anvil business like his father, and Lisette took up housekeeping alongside her mother-in-law. But she never really got used to the Midwest—too cold, too different, whatever. She always pined for New Orleans. To try to make her feel better, Maxwell built a solarium onto the back of the house—that's like a big greenhouse."

"Duh," Bess said. "We know what a solarium is."

George rolled her eyes. "Anyway, he had it planted

with palm trees and all kinds of other Gulf Coast type plants. He even brought in a big potted magnolia tree, since that was her favorite flower back home. She spent tons of time out there just wandering around and smelling the flowers—especially during those long Midwestern winters."

Bess gave a shiver. "I don't blame her," she said. "I'd like to have a southern solarium to hang out in myself, especially around February when we get our umpteenth foot of snow."

"So did they ever move back to New Orleans?" I asked. I'd heard some of the ghostly rumors about the Ayers place, of course, but hadn't paid much attention to the details. Like George, I didn't believe in ghosts.

"No," George said. "A few years passed, Maxwell and Lisette had a couple of kids, and they were still talking about going back. But before they managed it, Lisette died."

Bess gasped. "Oh, no!" she said. "How did she die?"

George shrugged. "I couldn't get a definite answer to that in my research," she said. "Some people claimed it was from a chill. Ironic, right? But other sources say she died in childbirth. Either way, the story is that to this day she remains a ghost trapped in the cold old house where she never really felt at home."

"Wow," Bess said. "That's sad."

"So why do people think the house is haunted?"

9

I asked. "I mean, I've always heard that it is. But have there been actual sightings?"

"I looked into that, too." George tapped her fingers on her camera. "Over the years, several people—neighbors mostly, or visitors, I guess—have claimed to hear riffs of jazz when no radio is playing, or catch a whiff of magnolia flowers when there are none around. Oh, and sometimes they say ordinary lights start flashing green, gold, and purple."

Bess looked perplexed. "What does that mean?"

"Mardi Gras colors." Ned glanced at her in the rearview. "Like Nancy's dress."

"Oh!" Bess said, nodding. "That's right."

"There were also reports of people seeing a lone, shadowy figure at an upstairs window gazing off toward the south," George said. "Or seeing the same figure in the solarium drifting around among the palms."

I turned and smiled at her. "Sounds like you're writing a pitch for that TV show *Ghostly Sightings*," I teased.

She grinned. "The thought has crossed my mind. It's all about marketing, right?"

Ned stopped at a red light and glanced over at me. "The whole story sounds like a mystery to me," he said with a wink. "Maybe you could solve it tonight, Nancy—the case of the cold ghost."

"Very funny." I'm pretty well known around town

for being an amateur detective. There's no case, large or small, that I won't tackle. But in my mind, ghost stories don't qualify. They're just that—stories. Nothing more.

Bess leaned forward to peer out the window. "We're almost there," she said, sounding excited.

I looked and spotted the old Ayers place halfway down the next block. It was handsome and dignified rising up in the center of the tree-lined street. Light poured out of every window downstairs, showing off the architectural details of the imposing facade. Cars were parked in almost every available spot along the curb, and people in Mardi Gras–style finery were laughing and chatting and hurrying toward the mansion. Even with the car windows shut, we could hear the lively jazz music drifting out into the night.

"Looks like you might be out of luck tonight, George," Ned said as we reached the house. "With all the lights and activity, the ghost will probably be hiding under the bed all night."

For once George didn't seem to have a retort. I glanced back and saw her staring out the side window. Her face had suddenly gone white beneath the blush and lipstick Bess had so carefully applied.

"What's wrong?" I asked.

"That!" George gasped, pointing out the window with a trembling finger.

2

Crowning Glory

I followed George's gaze. She was pointing to a couple around our own age climbing out of an expensive sports car just across from the mansion.

Bess had seen them as well. "Oh," she said. "It's Deirdre."

"Right." George made a face. "A scarier sight than any ghost."

To say that George and Deirdre Shannon don't get along is an understatement. Then again, Deirdre doesn't get along with much of anybody. She's what Hannah might call a piece of work. George prefers to call her something like the rude, spoiled rich girl who thinks she's better than everyone else.

As for me, I do my best to stay out of Deirdre's way. That's not always easy, though. He father is a successful attorney, just like mine, and sometimes that seems to give her the idea we're in competition with each other. Plus it doesn't help that she's had a crush on Ned for practically forever—not that she ever has any shortage of dates. She seems to have a new guy every other week.

"Wow, check out her amazing dress," Bess said.

George snorted. "I would, if I could stop staring at the ridiculous little crown she's wearing," she said. "Leave it to Deirdre! She must have finally declared herself Princess of the World."

I had to agree that Deirdre was dressed in an outfit that could only be called elaborate, even by Mardi Gras standards. Her gown was an ornate confection of gold brocade and champagne silk, with glass beads dangling here and there on the low-cut bodice and full skirt. She was holding a gold, heavily feathered cat's-eye mask on a crystal wand. Her hands were covered by silk gloves, and a jewel-encrusted tiara sparkled brightly atop her dark tresses. She really did look like royalty, which was probably exactly what she was going for.

Ned maneuvered the car into the last parking space on the block, just a couple of spots down from where Deirdre's masked date was parked. We all climbed out just as the pair walked by.

"Hello, Deirdre," Ned said. "How's it going, Adam?"

I blinked, belatedly recognizing Adam Fielding behind his mask. I'd known Adam forever, though I hadn't seen him since he'd left for college in Chicago the previous fall. I'd heard that he and Deirdre had been going out for over a month, which was practically a record for Deirdre. Like I said, she goes through boyfriends quickly.

"Hi, Adam," I said. "How's school?"

"Good," he replied. "I'm out on spring break this week, so I thought I'd come hang out in River Heights. And, uh, dress up like a complete dork," he added sheepishly, glancing down at his outfit. He was dressed to match Deirdre, in a black tuxedo with a gold cummerbund and a black-and-gold feathered mask. The whole thing was topped off with a long, black cape with champagne lining. It was a far cry from his usual understated preppy look.

"Don't be ridiculous, Adam," Deirdre said, reaching up to adjust a stray piece of his dark hair. "You look wonderful."

"I like your outfit, Deirdre," Bess said as we stepped into the street to cross over to the mansion. "It's very festive. And that tiara looks nice on you. Is it new?"

George coughed the words *stupid crown* into her hand. Deirdre raised one hand to gently touch the edge of the sparkling tiara.

"It's not mine," she said, ignoring George's

comment. "It belongs to Olde River Jewelers. Adam's father loaned it to me for tonight's event. We thought it was only appropriate, since the tiara has a history with Mardi Gras and this house." She smiled smugly. "It's gorgeous, isn't it? As soon as I saw it, I knew it would go perfectly with my outfit."

"A history with the Ayers place?" I asked Deirdre, curious. "What do you mean?"

Deirdre shrugged. "I don't know every little detail," she said with a touch of annoyance. "The important thing is, it works with the dress. It's like an old Ayers family heirloom or something, I guess."

Adam cleared his throat. "Actually, the tiara belonged to Mr. Ayers's grandmother, who brought it with her when she moved here from New Orleans. Her name was Lisette Ayers."

George gasped. "The ghost lady!" she blurted out.

"Ghosts?" Deirdre wrinkled her nose. "I knew you were pretty juvenile, Georgia. But I didn't realize you were a nutjob, too."

"Takes one to know one, *DeeDee*," George retorted, lingering over the nickname, which Deirdre hates just as much as George hates her own full name.

I ignored their bickering. "So the tiara was Lisette's?" I asked Adam. "How did your dad end up with it?" Adam's father owns the nicest jewelry store in town. He sells lots of antique stuff as well as regular jewelry, but I was still surprised to learn that he had the tiara. It didn't seem in character for Jackson Ayers to let an important family heirloom out of his hands.

Adam glanced around, as if to make sure nobody else was listening. "Well, I'm sure you know that Mr. Ayers has been having some, well, financial issues these past few years. After all, that's why we're all here tonight, right?"

"Oh." Now I understood. "So he sold the tiara to Olde River Jewelers in order to raise funds?"

"Something to do with replacing the plumbing, I think." Adam shrugged. "Anyway, it's been in the vault at the store ever since. I think the reason Dad didn't put it on display was because he thought it would make Mr. Ayers feel bad."

"That was nice of him," I said politely, though I wasn't quite convinced that that was why the tiara had stayed in the vault. Mr. Fielding hadn't built his jewelry shop into one of the most successful businesses in River Heights by making decisions based on personal sympathy. "So was the tiara—"

The rest of my question was swallowed up by the sudden deafening roar of a motor coming toward us. "Look out!" Ned shouted, grabbing my arm and yanking me over to the sidewalk.

A second later a black sports car zoomed past and

screeched to a halt in front of one of the neighbor's driveways. As soon as the motor cut off, the door swung open. The driver, a slim, short young man with dark hair, climbed out. It was hard to see much else, since he was wearing a black mask to match his old-fashioned tuxedo.

"Nice driving, bozo!" George called. "You could've killed us!"

The masked man strode toward us. "Who have we here?" he asked in a husky voice that practically oozed rebellion. He whipped off his mask, revealing an overly angular, but still good-looking face—a face I'd never seen before. "You're gorgeous, sweetheart!"

He was talking to Deirdre. Adam immediately stepped forward with a slight frown.

"I don't believe we've met," he said. "I'm Adam Fielding."

"Good for you." The stranger didn't take his eyes off Deirdre or acknowledge Adam's outstretched hand. "You know, I thought this party was going to be utterly and insufferably lame. But now I'm glad I'm here." He suddenly swept into a bow in front of Deirdre, practically brushing the ground with his hand. "I'm Derek. And you don't have to tell me who you are. I can already see that you're the most beautiful girl in the world."

Deirdre pursed her lips, looking amused—and

17

flattered. "Nice to meet you, Derek," she said. "I'm Deirdre."

She held out her hand. Derek kissed it. "Charmed and delighted," he pronounced.

I shot Bess an amused glance. Obviously this Derek, whoever he was, had a flair for the dramatic.

"Look, buddy," Adam said, stepping forward with a scowl. He reached out and poked the newcomer on the shoulder. "I'd appreciate it if you'd keep your hands off my date."

Derek smirked. "Oh, really? I don't hear her complaining. Why don't you let the lady speak for herself?"

Adam's hands clenched into fists at his sides. "I have a better idea—" he began.

Ned hurriedly stepped forward. "Guys, guys," he said soothingly. "This is supposed to be a party. Let's relax and remember we're here to have fun, okay?"

"You're right, Ned." Adam relaxed, then stepped over and put an arm around Deirdre's shoulders.

"Hey!" she complained, shrugging him off. "Watch it—it took two hours for Margaretta to do my hair this afternoon!"

"It was worth it, gorgeous," Derek told her, reaching over and quickly squeezing her hand. "See *you* inside."

With that, he took off across the street without a

word or a glance for the rest of us. A moment later he disappeared through the front door of the mansion.

"Interesting guy," George commented.

"He seems nice," Deirdre said with a self-satisfied smile. "I wonder why I've never seen him around. This town could use a few more people with his sense of . . . discernment." She let her gaze—and her smirk—wander over toward Bess.

I rolled my eyes. It didn't take a detective to figure out what she was thinking. Deirdre likes to think of herself as the prettiest girl in town, and the fact that Bess usually gets more male attention than she does has always bugged her big-time.

"Actually, he seemed like kind of a jerk to me." Adam was still scowling. "He'd better not get in my face again, or he'll regret it."

Bess smiled and touched his arm. "Don't let him get to you, Adam," she said. "It's obvious he was just trying to push your buttons."

"Yeah." Adam shook his head. "Maybe you're right, Bess. He's not worth it."

"That's the spirit. Now come on, people," Ned said. "Let's head inside. It's cold out here."

I shivered slightly, realizing he was right. A breeze had sprung up when the sun set, and the dampness left over from last night's rain made the air bone-chillingly cold.

19

"Let's go," I said, taking Ned's arm and heading up the front walk. The music was louder there, and I hummed along with the lively Dixieland tune.

I glanced up at the facade of the grand old mansion. Its redbrick exterior was luminous with a rich antique patina and bright white woodwork. The downstairs curtains were pulled back, allowing pockets of light to seep out onto the front lawn. Glancing up, I caught a flash of movement in one of the upstairs windows. I looked more closely, squinting at the window on the far left. As I did, a fragment of music drifted past my ears—not the loud, cheery party tune from inside, but a soft, jazzy, rather melancholy riff.

I tilted my head curiously, but the sound had faded. "Did you guys hear that?" I asked.

"Hear what?" George said, shifting her camera to her other hand.

I shook my head and smiled. "Never mind," I said, no longer certain I'd heard or seen anything. Maybe George's ghost stories were getting to me.

Soon we were plunging into the party. The big front rooms of the mansion were decked out in streamers, confetti, and balloons. I spotted Jackson Ayers standing near the door. He was decked out for the occasion too, in a snow-white suit with a green shirt and handkerchief, a gold tie, spats, a mask, and a purple top hat and cane. His face was glowing with excitement as he hurried toward us.

"Welcome, welcome, young people!" he sang out, a broad smile stretching across his thin face. "*Laissez les bons temps rouler*! That's a well-known New Orleans saying meaning 'Let the good times roll.'"

"Looks like you got a great turnout tonight, Mr. Ayers," Ned said, raising his voice to be heard above the music.

Jackson had just noticed Deirdre's tiara. His smile faded slightly, and a shadow passed over his face. But then he rubbed his hands together and glanced around the crowded room. "Yes, yes," he said. "It's so gratifying and humbling to know that so many people want to support this place. I hope we raise enough to repair the old solarium. Sadly, it's fallen into quite a state over these last few years."

"Oh, no!" George peered over his shoulder toward the hallways that led to the back of the house. "I've heard so much about the solarium—I was hoping to get a good look at it tonight."

"I'm afraid you can't do more than peep in through the windows," Jackson said, shaking his head. "Much of the glass is loose in its frames, and some of the panels are cracking, so it's completely off-limits for the time being. It's not safe enough for anyone to go inside until it's repaired."

George's face fell. "Oh, that's too bad," she mumbled.

As Jackson moved on to greet someone else, I grabbed George and pulled her aside. "Let me guess," I murmured. "You were planning to do some ghost busting in the solarium tonight?"

"It's a totally ghostly hot spot," George hissed back. "I mean, that's where Lisette spent most of her time, according to the stories. And there have been tons of mysterious sightings there. I'm sure I could get some spooky photos."

Deirdre and Adam had wandered off, and Ned was talking to one of his professors nearby, but Bess had overheard. "George," she said sternly, "promise us you won't try to sneak in there tonight."

I nodded. "You heard what Mr. Ayers said. It's not safe."

"That's interesting coming from you, Nancy." George scowled at me. "You're the one who's always sneaking into dangerous places when you're on the trail of some mystery or other."

"That's different," I said.

"Promise us!" Bess added warningly.

George rolled her eyes. "All right, all right. I promise. I'm sure I can find something spooky to photograph in the rest of the house."

"That's the spirit," I said, then giggled as I realized what I'd said. "No pun intended."

Just then Adam's father, Mr. Fielding, spotted me and hurried over. He was dressed as a nineteenth-century Southern gentleman, complete with a big gold pocket watch bouncing against his portly belly. "Nancy Drew!" he exclaimed. "Nice to see you here. Is Carson around?"

"Hi, Mr. Fielding," I said. "No, Dad couldn't make it tonight. He's out of town on business."

"Ah, too bad he has to miss it. Well, enjoy the party."

Ned, Bess, and I continued to circulate for the next few minutes. Practically everyone we knew was there, from Mayor Simmons and her family to Chief McGinnis of the River Heights Police Department. Even half of my old elementary school teachers had shown up! Almost everyone had thrown themselves into the spirit of the theme, dressing up in gowns or formal suits, or wearing jester costumes or other traditional outfits. Most also wore fancy masks decorated with feathers, glitter, or Mardi Gras beads.

George stayed with us, but I could tell she was distracted. She kept fiddling with her camera and glancing toward the back of the house.

"Hey, is that a ghost over there?" I whispered to her. "Oops! No, sorry. It's just a curtain."

"Very funny," George replied.

Bess giggled. "I see one! Quick, George, take a picture! Oops, never mind. It's just Mrs. Mahoney."

George made a face at her. "Just wait until something really mysterious happens," she said. "That's when I—"

CRASH!

The floor shook as a loud sudden noise cut off the rest of whatever George was about to say. It had come from the upstairs—directly over our heads.

Looking for Trouble

George was sprinting toward the steps before the echo faded, her camera clutched in one hand and her skirt gathered up out of the way with the other. "Be back soon!" she called over her shoulder.

Bess chuckled. "Think she'll catch any ghosts?"

"I don't know," Ned said. "Do ghosts usually push over vases? Because that's what it sounded like."

"I thought ghosts didn't have real bodies," I said with a smile. "Isn't that how they drift through walls? How could they push over a vase, even if they wanted to?"

"I think you're right." Bess glanced upward. "It was probably just a clumsy party guest."

All around us, other guests were buzzing about the sudden noise. Some of them drifted in the direction

25

of the steps while others pressed back near the front door looking slightly nervous. I wondered if people were more worried about the ghost stories or the house's general state of disrepair.

"I think I'll take advantage of this distraction to grab some refreshments," Ned said.

"I'll come with you," Bess said.

I suddenly felt thirsty myself, but something was distracting me. "Bring me a soda, okay?" I'd just noticed Adam doing his best to hustle Deirdre out the nearby side door. I wandered a little closer as my friends took off through the crowd. I wasn't trying to be nosy, but I was curious.

"Forget it!" Deirdre's annoyed voice rose over the hubbub of the party. "Are you insane? I'm not going outside because some clumsy dork knocked something over upstairs. The wind will mess up my hair."

"Just for a minute," Adam said. "You know, until we're sure things are safe."

"Grow up, Adam." Deirdre rolled her eyes dramatically. "I never realized you were such a chicken." She reached up with one hand to adjust her tiara, and then tilted her chin up. "Now, if you'll excuse me, I'm going over to say hello to Mr. Halloran. He's one of Daddy's most important clients, you know."

She swept off toward the other end of the room. Adam's shoulders slumped as he watched her go.

I couldn't help feeling a twinge of sympathy. It had to be difficult dating Deirdre sometimes—*most* of the time, probably.

"Hey, Adam," I said in a friendly voice, walking over to him. "Enjoying the party so far?"

He blinked at me. "Oh, hi again, Nancy," he said, tilting his mask up onto his head. "Sure, it's great. How about you?"

"Definitely. I'm glad so many people are here tonight. The fund-raiser looks like quite a success." I shot a quick look up at the ceiling; several sets of footsteps were faintly audible from upstairs. "I just hope nothing important was broken just now."

Adam smiled faintly, glancing up as well. "I wonder if that was the Ayers ghost."

"Hey, you never know." I laughed. For some reason, that little burst of melancholy music I'd heard outside—or *thought* I'd heard—flashed into my mind. But I shook off the thought as quickly as it came.

Adam turned to stare at Deirdre, who was chatting animatedly with a group of people near the front door. I cleared my throat, feeling awkward and sort of wishing I hadn't come over. Adam clearly had it bad. I scanned my mind for a handy bit of small talk.

"So, Adam," I said, "what are you doing this summer? Coming home to work for your dad at the store again?"

He grimaced. "Not if I can help it," he said. "Actually, I'm planning to spend most of the summer break in London." His expression brightened as he spoke. "A buddy of mine up at school knows about a flat we can rent, and a bunch of us are going in on it together. Maybe Deirdre, too, if I can talk her into it."

"Sounds like fun." I smiled politely. Yep, he definitely had it bad if he actually believed he and Deirdre would still be together by summer. After all, that was still months away. Obviously poor Adam hadn't yet figured out that Deirdre's relationships rarely lasted longer than her haircuts. "Oh, there's George—excuse me, I need to go talk to her."

"Sure. See you around." Adam's gaze had already returned to Deirdre.

George emerged from the back hallway where the stairs were. She saw me and hurried over, still clutching her camera.

"Get any ghost photos?" I asked, doing my best to keep a straight face.

George shook her head. "No supernatural forces involved this time, unfortunately," she said. "It was just that obnoxious Derek guy. Remember—from outside?"

"You mean Deirdre's not-so-secret admirer? How could I forget?" I joked. "What did he knock over?"

"A lamp," George said. "He claims he didn't have

anything to do with it, but I saw him earlier, lurking around on the balcony outside Lisette's old bedroom." She shrugged. "It was definitely him. Nobody else was even upstairs when I got there."

I smiled. "I don't know. Sounds like circumstantial evidence to me."

"Thanks, Detective Drew," George said. But her smile faded as she watched Derek himself come down the stairs and wade into the crowd. "Actually, it's probably a really good thing you're here. That way you can take the case if anything just happens to mysteriously disappear while that jerk is around." She looked meaningfully toward Derek, then around the antique-filled room.

I chuckled. "Don't worry. If anything suspicious happens, I bet Adam will be more than willing to question Derek for us."

I glanced over to where I'd last seen Adam, but he'd already disappeared. The party was getting more crowded by the minute, and I couldn't even see Deirdre anymore.

"There you are!" Bess exclaimed, hurrying toward us with Ned at her heels. They were each carrying two sodas. Bess handed one to George, and I took the other from Ned. "It's so packed in here we practically had to send out a search party."

Just then a new song started, a lilting, jazzy waltz.

29

Ned hummed along, tapping his foot. "Enough ghost talk," he said. His mask had been perched on top of his head, making his hair stick out. He snapped it back over his face and held out his arm to me. "Life is for the living, and I feel like dancing. Shall we, lovely lady?"

I took his arm. "We shall, mysterious sir."

George rolled her eyes. "Oh, please."

Ned and I swept out onto the dance floor and found a spot among the couples already spinning and dipping. The two of us had danced together countless times, but somehow it felt extra special tonight. The dress, the masks, the jazz, the mansion, and the Mardi Gras spirit—I'm not overly romantic, but I'll admit I was falling under a little bit of a spell. I closed my eyes and leaned against Ned, wondering if this was what it had felt like when Maxwell Ayers and Lisette first danced together way down south in New Orleans. . . .

"Excuse us!" Deirdre's voice rang out over the music. She was elbowing her way to the center of the dance floor with Adam in tow. A few other couples backed off, looking startled.

"Looks like those two made up," I whispered into Ned's ear.

Ned followed my gaze. "You mean after the Derek incident?"

"That, too," I said with a shrug. "They had a bit of a tiff a few minutes ago."

Deirdre was wearing her usual smug smile. Even with the loud music pouring out of the speakers, her voice carried as she talked to her partner.

"Have you noticed all the attention my outfit is getting?" she was saying. "I mean, this dress is pretty spectacular all on its own. But you were totally right, Adam—the tiara just pulls the whole look together. Although, Margaretta also deserves a tiny bit of credit—if she hadn't been able to pull off the hair-style I told her to . . ."

There was more, but I wasn't listening. My eyes widened as I spotted Derek pushing his way between dancers, making a beeline for Deirdre and Adam.

"Uh-oh," I muttered. "Here comes trouble."

Derek's black mask covered much of his face, but it was easy to see that his gaze was focused on Deirdre. He swept into a deep bow in front of her.

"May I cut in?" It didn't really come out as a question so much as a command.

Deirdre simpered. "Oh, I don't know . . . ," she began with a giggle.

"Get lost, buddy," Adam growled, spinning Deirdre around to block her from Derek with his own body. "She's with me."

"There you go again," Derek said. "Making the

lady's decisions for her. Afraid of what she'll decide on her own?"

This time Adam let go of Deirdre and turned to face Derek straight on. Adam was quite a bit taller, not to mention broader through the shoulders. A few of the couples dancing nearby shot the two guys nervous glances and moved a little farther away. Bess looked over at me and widened her eyes with concern.

"Yikes," I whispered to Ned. "If Derek doesn't back down . . ."

Ned nodded grimly. "Yeah," he murmured. "Adam's always had a bit of a temper, and it looks like he's at his breaking point."

"Look, dude," Adam said. "You seem a little slow on the uptake, so let me spell it out for you. She's. Not. Interested."

Deirdre rolled her eyes. "Oh, Adam," she said disdainfully. "You don't have to get all macho about it. Please."

Adam ignored her, still glowering at Derek. "Leave us alone."

"Are you going to make me?" Derek retorted, stepping closer.

Ned hurried over before Adam could respond. "Guys, guys," he said quickly. "Let's not cause a scene here, okay?"

I grabbed Deirdre and pulled her aside. It was pretty obvious that she wasn't going to help. She was probably enjoying all the extra attention too much.

"This is supposed to be Mr. Ayers's night, not yours," I reminded her. "I don't want your dysfunctional love life to mess this up for him."

"Whatever." Deirdre rolled her eyes. "All this drama is getting really tired," she announced loudly. "I'm going to powder my nose."

She swept off toward the back of the house, pushing her way between dancers.

I went over to Bess. "That was interesting, wasn't it?"

Bess nodded toward the guys. "Looks like Ned got things simmered down, at least."

Sure enough, the fight appeared to have fizzled out. Derek was rolling his eyes at Ned, and Adam was staring moodily after Deirdre, who was still pushing her way toward the back of the room.

"Think I'll step outside for some air," Adam said loudly. "Maybe someone can let Deirdre know when she gets back." Spinning on his heels, he stalked off in the direction of the side doors.

"Whoa," Derek said. "That dude's really tense." He glanced around, and his gaze fixed on Bess. "Hey, beautiful," he said. "Looks like you need someone to dance with."

"Actually, I'm fine by myself," Bess said coolly.

"Trust me, sweetheart," Derek said. "You *want* to dance with me." He took her hand.

Bess yanked it back. "No, thank you," she said, her voice practically dripping ice water. "I'd rather not."

"Let's go get some more drinks," I suggested, taking Ned's hand.

"You go ahead," Bess waved. "I can handle this." She nodded her head toward Derek.

As entertaining as it would have been to watch Bess cut Derek down to size, all that dancing and drama had made me thirsty. Besides, Bess had always known how to handle obnoxious guys.

Soon Ned and I were making our way through the crowded main room. Right by the French doors that lead to the side porch, a table of New Orleans–style delicacies and cups filled with punch had been set up.

"Quite a spread, isn't it?"

I glanced up to see Evaline Waters smiling at me. "Oh, hello, Ms. Waters," I said with a smile. Evaline Waters is one of my favorite people in River Heights. She's a retired librarian with a quick smile and an infectious zest for life. "This is a great party, isn't it?"

"Wonderful," Ms. Waters agreed. Her salt-and-pepper hair was tucked up under a fancy hat that matched her dress. "And your outfit is spectacular,

Nancy." She sighed happily. "I'm so glad dear Jackson agreed to this fund-raiser. This really is an incredible old house. Have you had a chance to look around? You shouldn't miss the gorgeous stained glass window in the back hall off the kitchen."

Ned handed me a cup off the table and took one for himself. "We'll be sure to take a look at that, Ms. Waters," he said. "Thanks for the tip."

We chatted with her for another moment or two before we excused ourselves.

"How about it?" I asked Ned. "Should we go check out that window?"

"Sure. She said it's right next to the entrance to the solarium, right?" Ned chuckled. "We should probably take a peek in there, too. I haven't seen George in quite a while. Knowing her, she probably sneaked in and got conked on the head by a falling pane of glass."

"Don't even say that," I groaned, only half kidding. "Come on, let's go."

We strolled off toward the back of the house and soon found the stained glass window, which really was impressive. Unlike the solarium, the window looked like it was still in pretty good condition. I glanced in through the rickety French doors at the back of the house. The solarium was an immense space lit only by the reflected light of the house and the dim shine of the moon and stars. A couple of large, drooping palms and a handful of smaller plants were all that remained of the lush Southern garden that George had described earlier.

As I squinted through the cloudy glass, trying to imagine what the solarium had looked like in its glory days, my eyes widened in surprise. A ghostly figure had just swept down the pathway!

In the Dark

I **grabbed Ned's arm. "Look!"** I hissed. "Someone's in there!"

My first glimpse of the figure through the wavy old glass had made it look ethereal and insubstantial. But as it moved closer, I saw that it was merely human after all. It was a woman in a white dress.

Ned stepped over to look. "And it's *not* George," he said.

"She's coming this way." Something made me whisper and pull Ned around the corner out of sight. Then I peered back out. I guess maybe I didn't want the woman—whoever it was—to think we'd been spying on her. When she emerged from the solarium, she didn't even glance in our direction. She was staring down the hall the opposite way.

"What were you doing in there, Patricia?" a new voice asked from that end of the hall.

"Was that Jackson's voice?" Ned breathed into my ear.

I nodded. Our host had just stepped into view, a slight frown on his face. And now I realized who the woman in white was—Patricia Ayers Ardmore, Jackson's niece and closest living relative. Patricia was about forty-five years old and married to hyper-successful real estate developer Bryan Ardmore. They lived in a fancy new house that Bryan had built for them after he'd turned an old dairy farm into a million-dollar subdivision called Ardmore Acres. I knew Patricia because her daughter, Maureen, had been a few years ahead of me in school.

"I was just taking a look around," Patricia told her uncle.

"You're not supposed to be in the solarium. It's not safe." Jackson shook his head. "The contractor said those panes could go at any moment."

"Right. Just like the wiring could go at any moment, and the roof could go at any moment." Patricia crossed her arms over her chest. "Why won't you face facts, Uncle Jackson? This place is a money pit. Always has been. It's foolish to keep clinging to it. Applying to get it on the Antique Homes Registry is just foolish—once it's on there, you'll never be able to sell it with all their restrictions!"

"I don't want to have this conversation again, Patricia." Jackson sounded stern. "This house is my home. I don't care how many condos that husband of yours thinks he can pack into it or how many of his modern monstrosities he could build on the extra land. I'm not selling."

Patricia sighed loudly and rolled her eyes heavenward. "Why do I even try to talk sense into you?" she exclaimed. "It's only because I care about you! This is supposed to be the family home, right? So why can't you let the rest of the family in on this decision? We worry about you living here all alone, Uncle Jackson, always worrying about making ends meet. It keeps me up at night sometimes!"

Jackson's expression had softened and he was patting Patricia on the arm. "Don't worry so much about the money, Patricia. I'm taking care of things," he told her reassuringly. "After tonight, we won't have to worry about money for quite a while."

I glanced up at Ned and motioned down the hall. We tiptoed away, the sounds of Jackson and Patricia's voices fading rapidly.

"Whew!" Ned said once we were safely back in the main room. "That was kind of awkward."

I nodded, twirling my mask. "Sounds like an argument they've had more than once," I said.

"There you guys are." Bess hurried toward us, holding up her long skirt with both hands. "I only managed to ditch Derek about two minutes ago. He just doesn't take 'get lost, jerk' for an answer!"

I grinned. "Sorry about that. But I knew you could handle him."

"Barely." Bess rolled her eyes. "So where's George?"

"We haven't seen her in a while," Ned said. "She's probably still looking for ghosts."

I'd just noticed Deirdre and Adam standing together a few yards away talking to some other guests. "Looks like those two made up again," I commented.

"Yeah, they both turned up a few minutes ago and started acting like nothing ever happened." Bess glanced over at the pair, then back at me. "Did you notice anything different about Deirdre?"

"What?" I joked. "You mean the way she looks even snootier than ever now that she has two guys fighting over her?"

"Some detective you are, Nancy." Bess laughed. "Didn't you see she's been decrowned?"

I blinked, realizing Bess was right. The glittery tiara was missing from Deirdre's dark hair.

"So what happened to the fancy tiara?" Ned asked. "She seemed so proud of that thing."

"I don't know," Bess said. "Let's go find out."

We took a few steps closer. Soon we could hear Deirdre's voice, which as usual was louder than it really needed to be.

". . . and so I rushed to the ladies' room and took it off," she was exclaiming dramatically to a pair of older women in beaded gowns. "I just hope I got it off in time—my scalp is still tingling from where it was pinching me. I have *very* sensitive skin, you know."

The older women cooed and clucked sympathetically. Beside her, Adam smiled vaguely, his gaze wandering around the room. Knowing Deirdre, she'd probably spent a good amount of time blabbing to anyone who would listen about her reasons for removing the tiara. Even listening to George expound on the latest computer software upgrade was more interesting than that!

Deirdre reached up and patted her hair. "It was yanking at my hair, too," she told the women. "I just was *not* going to put up with that all evening, you know? The tiara may be special and all that, but this is my skin and hair we're talking about." She waved one hand airily. "So I just took the thing off and stuck it in my purse. I decided it didn't even look that good anyway. It was actually sort of distracting, really."

Bess and I shared a look of amusement. Leave it to

41

Deirdre—even a valuable antique tiara wasn't good enough for her!

"Mystery solved," I joked to Bess and Ned. "Should we—"

Before I could finish, the lights flickered out and the music cut off.

It was nearly pitch black in the room. Several people screamed, and a low hubbub of confused voices filled the silence.

"What's going on?" someone shouted.

"Is it the ghost?" another voice shrieked giddily. Laughter bubbled up from various directions. I glanced over at Ned, who was little more than a shadowy blob. It was surprising just how dark it was with the power off—only a handful of flickering candles on the fireplace mantle and the large rectangles of the windows offered any light.

"All right, everyone!" I recognized Chief McGinnis's voice rising over the rest. "Let's just stay calm. I'm sure we'll get this sorted out in a moment."

"That's right." Jackson's quavery voice spoke up next. "I'm very sorry about this, friends. It seems the old wiring isn't what it used to be."

Beside me, I heard Bess clear her throat. "If someone has a flashlight, I'd be happy to take a look at the circuit box."

"There's a flashlight in the kitchen," Jackson said. "Perhaps if someone near the hall could—"

He was interrupted by a burst of static. The lights flickered briefly, and a few bars of tinny music drifted through the room, fading in and out. I recognized the tune—it was "When the Saints Go Marching In."

"Weird," Ned muttered.

Before I could respond, the lights flickered again, then came back on for good. Cheers rose from the crowd.

Glancing around, I saw that most people were smiling or laughing. "Good one, Jackson!" a man called out, raising his glass. "Very convincing."

"Yeah," someone else cried. "I could have sworn I saw the ghost of Lisette coming to get me!"

"They think he did it on purpose," I pointed out. "Taking advantage of all those old ghost stories to add spice to the party."

"Maybe they're right," Bess said, though she sounded doubtful.

Ned shook his head. "If so, it was a pretty careless stunt," he said disapprovingly. "Someone could've been hurt."

I had to agree. "If Jackson did do it on purpose, he'd better not admit that to Chief McGinnis," I said.

"He doesn't have much of a sense of humor about stuff like that."

"Hey! What was that all about?" George had just appeared in the doorway behind us. "Who turned out the lights just now?"

"Where have you been?" Bess asked her. "I was starting to think the ghost got you."

"I was upstairs looking arou—"

"Nancy! There you are." Deirdre's loud voice cut off George's words. "I need to talk to you. Privately."

She grabbed my arm and yanked at it so hard she almost made me drop my mask.

"What is it, Deirdre?" I asked. "I'm kind of in the middle of something right now."

"Trust me, this can't wait." She glared at me, as if daring me to contradict her.

I sighed. When Deirdre gets like that, it's usually more trouble than it's worth to argue with her.

"Be right back, guys," I told my friends.

Deirdre took me out on the side porch. It was dark and chilly, so we had the place to ourselves. With the doors shut, the music from inside was muffled enough for me to hear the peaceful sounds of frogs and insects chirping. I wrapped my arms around myself for warmth as Deirdre turned to face me.

"What's this all about?" I asked. "If you're looking

for a little girl talk about which of your two guys is hunkier, I'm really not—"

"Don't be stupid," Deirdre snapped. "Why would I talk to someone like you about something like that?"

"What, then?" I was rapidly losing patience with her.

She took a deep breath. "It's about that tiara," she blurted out. "It's not really in my purse like I've been telling everybody. It's been stolen!"

5

Whodunit

My eyes widened. **"Stolen?"** I repeated. "Did they try to take the whole purse, or just the tiara?"

"No, no!" Deirdre waved her arms around in annoyance. "Keep up, will you? I never had it in my purse at all."

I blinked, confused. "Wait," I said. "Start again, okay? What happened to the tiara?"

Deirdre started wringing her hands and pacing around the creaky old porch. "It happened when I went to the restroom earlier," she said. "After Adam and that other guy were fighting over dancing with me, remember?" A brief expression of self-satisfaction crossed her face before the worried crease in her forehead returned. "Anyway, I was in there touching up my lipstick when the lights went out."

"Wait," I said, more confused than ever. "You mean you were still in the bathroom when the lights cut off just now?"

"No, no!" Deirdre threw her hands in the hair. "I thought you were supposed to be, like, smart? Maybe Adam was right—I shouldn't have told you anything about it."

I mustered every last ounce of my patience. Whatever she was trying to tell me, it definitely sounded like something I needed to know. "I'm sorry," I said soothingly. "Go on—please. So you're saying the lights went out earlier, too?"

Deirdre nodded. "At least the lights in the bathroom did. I could see a little bit of light coming in under the door. Anyway, before I could scream, someone grabbed me from behind and covered my mouth."

I gasped, startled in spite of myself. "Really?" I said. "What happened after they grabbed you?"

"They yanked the tiara right off my head." Deirdre touched her hair gently as she spoke. "Practically tore out half my hair by the roots, too. It was horrible."

"Did the thief say anything?" I asked.

She shook her head. "Not a word. But he shoved a piece of paper in my hand. Then he let go of me and ran out of the room. The lights came back on a second later."

"What was on the paper?"

"Here. See for yourself." She reached into the hem of her glove, pulled out a folded scrap of paper, and handed it over.

I squinted to read it in the dim light. The paper was small, about the size of a dollar bill. There were a bunch of tiny words printed on it, but it was too dark to make them out.

"It says I have to come up with the full value of the tiara in cash by the end of the party tonight," Deirdre said. "If I don't—or if I so much as breathe a word about this to the police—I'll never see it again!" She bit her lip and started pacing again. "And if that happens, I'm going to have to come up with something to tell Mr. Fielding. I definitely do *not* want to deal with that!"

I was still peering at the note. "What are you supposed to do with the money if you get it?"

"I don't know." She waved one hand. "It says something about being contacted when the time is right. But that's not the point! There's no way I can get that much cash in the next few hours—not without telling anyone what's going on, anyway." She stopped short and glared at me. "So you've *got* to help me figure out who did this! And you'd better do it fast!"

Although I wasn't crazy about the way Deirdre was bossing me around, I hated the thought that such a historically valuable tiara had fallen into criminal hands. Besides, I can't resist a good mystery. Of course I was going to do my best to help Deirdre get the tiara back.

I folded the note carefully and stuck it in my purse. "Okay," I said. "Who else knows about this?"

"Nobody," Deirdre said. "Well, except Adam, I mean." She rolled her eyes. "I'm not about to go blabbing it around, if that's what you're driving at." She grabbed my arm. "And you can't either! You won't tell Chief McGinnis, will you? Swear it!"

"Relax," I assured her. "I won't tell him." I felt a twinge of guilt at the thought that I was about to start investigating this crime right under the police chief's nose, but I pushed it aside. If the police found out about this, the thief was likely to disappear with the tiara as threatened, and that would be that.

"Good." Deirdre looked mollified. "Okay, then it's our secret, right?"

"Sure," I said. "I might need to bring my friends in on it too, though. We don't have much time, and I may need their help."

"Your friends?" Deirdre sounded dubious.

I decided not to give her a chance to start complaining about that. "So you didn't see who grabbed you at all? Not even in the mirror as he was leaving?"

"Not really. It was dark, remember?" She shivered

slightly. "It looked like a guy in a black mask. That's all I could tell. And I'm not even totally sure about that."

"Okay." Her mention of the black mask made me think immediately of Derek. He certainly wasn't the only one at the party wearing a plain black mask with his costume. But he was the only one who didn't seem to know anyone at the party. Why had he come, anyway?

"What?" Deirdre demanded, watching me carefully. "What are you thinking about?"

"We'd better get back inside. If the thief sees us together out here, he might figure out what's up—especially if he knows about my reputation for solving mysteries."

"Oh, please." Deirdre rolled her eyes. "It's not like you're some kind of celebrity, Nancy. I bet half the people at the country club don't even know who you are."

But she didn't protest as I led the way back inside. It felt warm and almost stuffy in there after being outside.

"Be sure to let me know what you find out!" Deirdre hissed. Then she hurried off toward Adam, who was standing near the catering table fiddling with the edge of his cape.

I spotted Bess and Ned chatting nearby. "So what

was the big emergency?" Ned asked when I joined them. "Did Deirdre break a nail or something?"

Bess laughed.

I smiled distractedly. "Listen, Bess," I said. "That guy Derek—did you say he was with you the whole time Ned and I were gone?"

"Stuck to me like glue. After a while I started calling him Velcro Boy, and he still didn't take the hint! I wasn't able to shake him until right before I saw you—and then it was only because Maureen Ardmore and some friend of hers came up and started flirting with him."

"Hmm." I bit my lip. According to Deirdre's story, the theft must have happened within ten minutes of when I'd left Bess with Derek on the dance floor—right after Deirdre left to go powder her nose. Ned and I had returned just before the housewide blackout, and at that point Bess had only ditched Derek a few minutes earlier. That meant there was no way he could have been the dark figure in the bathroom—he was with Bess the whole time.

"What's up, Nancy?" Ned raised an eyebrow. "If I didn't know better, I'd think you had that look in your eye."

Bess gasped. "Oh my gosh, you're right! Nancy? Did you actually manage to come up with a mystery while we weren't looking?"

I grinned sheepishly. "Sort of," I said. "That's what Deirdre wanted to talk to me about." After checking to make sure nobody else was close enough to over-hear, I filled them in on the case. I also showed them the note—hiding it behind my cupped palms—and took a better look at it myself:

By the end of the party tonight,
u must come up with the full value
of the tiara—in cash! Do NOT tell
the police—I am watching u. If u
so much as breathe a word of this
to the police, u can consider ur
precious tiara gone forever!
U will be contacted when
the time is right.

"I get it," Bess said, squinting at the tiny letters. "So the first suspect on your list was Mr. Short, Dark, and Pushy."

Ned nodded. "It makes sense. He's the only guest tonight who seems to be a stranger to everybody else, and he seems pretty sketchy."

"Only it doesn't work," I said, quickly outlining my thoughts about the timeline. "He couldn't have done it. Not unless he has an accomplice, someone he's working with who did it for him."

Bess glanced around. "Well, we know everybody else here," she pointed out. "I guess someone could have sneaked in just long enough to grab the tiara."

"Seems a little far-fetched, but you never know," I said. "Come on, let's go take a look at the scene of the crime."

Remembering what Deirdre had said about the bathroom being under the stairs, I headed for the central hallway. The staircase twisted around itself, and the area around it was just as poorly lit as Deirdre had described. Tucked into an alcove beneath the first twist of the stairway was a plain wooden door with a sign hanging on it. The sign read COME ON IN, and when I reached up to flip it over, the other side said OCCUPIED—PLEASE WAIT.

"Good thing that sign is there," Bess said. "There's no lock on the bathroom door."

Leaning closer, I saw that she was right.

"Check this out." Ned flipped a switch on the wall nearby, causing the bathroom light to flash on behind the door. "The light switch is outside the bathroom."

"That's an old house for you," Bess said. "My grandma's house has a bathtub in the kitchen."

I rubbed my chin. "Guess that explains how the bad guy cut the lights. Pretty convenient."

"Yeah. No ghostly forces necessary," Bess added, clearly thinking about the big blackout. She pushed open the bathroom door and reached inside. The light went off, then on again. "There's another switch in here. I guess you can work the lights from inside or out."

"Speaking of ghostly forces, where's George?" I asked, realizing that she'd disappeared again.

Bess shrugged. "I haven't seen her in a while."

I fought back a flash of annoyance. There wasn't much time to solve this—George would be much more useful helping us investigate than off doing her silly ghost hunting. Still, I reminded myself that I wasn't being fair—she had no idea what was going on yet.

"Okay, so we know *how* the thief did it," I said, wandering into the bathroom and staring around. It was a fairly ordinary powder room, except for the strange location of the light switch. "But we're still no closer to figuring out *who* did it. Aside from Derek, I can only think of a couple of possibilities, but they seem kind of . . ."

I let my voice trail off as Ned cleared his throat loudly. He nodded his head meaningfully toward the arched doorway leading from the main room into the stairway hall. "Incoming," he murmured.

Stepping out of the bathroom and glancing over, Adam Fielding was walking into the stairwell area. "Hi, Nancy," he said. "Um, I was just talking to

Deirdre. She said you might tell your friends, um, you know, what she told you?"

"We all know, Adam," Bess spoke up. "I guess Deirdre told you, too?"

I realized I'd forgotten to mention that part to Bess and Ned. "Don't worry," I told Adam. "We're on the case."

"Okay. Um, but I was thinking." He glanced around and lowered his voice. "What if it was someone from outside? I mean, a lot of people knew that Deirdre would be wearing the Ayers tiara tonight." He smiled ruefully. "She hasn't exactly been keeping it a secret, you know? So maybe someone figured this would be a good time to swipe it. Whoever it was could've sneaked in, grabbed it, and then blacked out all the lights a few minutes later to get away." He shrugged. "If that's the case, he's probably long gone by now."

"That's an interesting theory," I said politely. "Thanks, Adam. We'll add it to the list."

"You're welcome." Adam smiled bashfully. "Just trying to help." He sighed. "Like I said, though, it may be hopeless. I really don't know how my dad is going to react if Deirdre doesn't come up with that ransom in time."

"Don't give up yet, man," Ned said, reaching over to pat Adam on the shoulder. "Nancy's on the case now. She's never met a crime she couldn't solve."

Adam nodded, though he didn't look too convinced. "Keep me posted, okay?" he said. Then he hurried off back to the main room.

"Do you think Adam is on to something?" Bess asked.

"It's possible, but I doubt it," I replied. "It just seems a little too unlikely. The thief would not only have to know about Deirdre wearing the tiara, but they'd also have to know about the bathroom not having a lock, and this funny light." I reached over and toggled the outside switch.

"And who from the outside would know about the lock, or the light switch?" Ned asked.

I nodded. "Exactly. Anyone who'd been at the party for more than a few minutes might know all that, but the only way someone from outside would have been able to plan the theft in advance would be if they'd seen the funny layout of the bathroom on a house tour or something." I thought about that for a moment, and then realized another flaw in the theory. "Besides, that person would already have had to sneak past everyone to get in without a ticket to the fund-raiser," I pointed out. "Why bother with the blackout to get out again?"

"Well, we still don't know for sure whether Jackson or another guest was behind the big blackout,"

Ned pointed out. "It could've been just for fun and thrills, like everyone seemed to assume."

"We should probably look into that." I bit my lip. "You know, I kind of wish Deirdre hadn't told Adam about this."

"Why?" Bess asked in surprise. "You don't think *he* did it, do you?"

"No, but what about his father?" I twirled my mask thoughtfully on its stick. "I'm sure Olde River Jewelers has that tiara insured for big money. It would be an obvious motive."

Ned and Bess exchanged a skeptical glance. "Mr. Fielding?" Ned said. "It seems unlikely he would do something like that. He's a respected member of the community. He's lived in River Heights most of his life."

"I know," I said. "But money makes people do crazy things sometimes—things you would never expect."

"I guess that's true," Bess admitted. "But I still have trouble believing that someone like Mr. Fielding would risk it."

I knew she was probably right. But I wasn't going to cross anyone off my suspect list until I knew more. "Come on, let's go back out and start investigating."

"Good idea," Ned agreed. "I could use something to drink, too."

We headed into the main room. "You brought me a drink last time," I told Ned with a smile. "I'll go get you one this time."

Leaving him with Bess near the entrance, I headed for the catering table. There was an enormous crystal punch bowl right in the middle of it. There was nobody near it at the moment, so I grabbed a couple of cups and reached for the scoop sticking out of the bowl.

Then I glanced down and froze. Staring up at me from the punch bowl was a pale, eyeless face!

6

Mask Task

It's a mask, I realized, my heart beginning to slow down to normal again. Floating lifelessly in the bloodred lake of punch, that mask was an eerie sight.

A pudgy middle-aged woman walked up just then and let out a shriek. "What *is* that?" she cried loudly enough to make everyone within a twenty-foot radius turn and look. She pointed into the punch bowl with a trembling finger.

Bess and Ned came hurrying over. "What's going on?" Bess asked breathlessly.

"Looks like someone's mask got into the punch bowl," I said.

Just then Jackson Ayers arrived. "What's wrong?" he asked. Then he looked down at the punch bowl.

"Oh, my!" he exclaimed. "That's one of Grandmother Lisette's old masks. How did it get in there?"

I reached in and gingerly picked up the mask. It was made mostly of white feathers, with a few sparkly beads sewn in. The edges swooped up and out in a dramatic cat's-eye shape. Fortunately the top of the mask had stayed mostly dry, though the edges of some of the feathers were stained pink from the punch.

"I hope it's not ruined," I said, handing it to Jackson. "Are you sure it was one of your grandmother's masks?"

I watched him carefully. His eyes were worried but guileless as he answered.

"I'm positive, Nancy," he said, carefully shaking some of the moisture from the old mask. "It was hanging in her room upstairs. I don't know why anyone would do such a thing."

"I remember seeing those masks in Lisette's bedroom when the garden club took your tour last fall, Jackson," the pudgy woman said. "It was a lovely display. Very festive."

"Thank you, Cora." Jackson bowed slightly and smiled. "I'm so sorry if you were startled. You too, Nancy. I can't apologize enough."

The woman giggled and blushed. "No, no, don't be silly," she said. "It was all in good fun."

As she wandered away, I realized she thought this had been nothing but another atmospheric party trick. But looking at Jackson's face as he stared down at the mask in his hand, I couldn't quite believe that he'd done it. He looked troubled and confused.

"I found these masks in an old trunk up in the attic years ago," he said, though he seemed to be talking to himself as much as to me or anyone else. He turned the white feather mask over in his wrinkled old hands. "I hung them up in Grandmother Lisette's bedroom even before I started giving historical tours of this old place. I thought that if her ghost really was hanging about like everyone thought, she might like to see them there . . . maybe remind her of happier days."

His voice trailed off and he stared down at the mask, seeming lost in thought. I exchanged a glance with Bess and Ned, pretty sure that they were thinking what I was thinking. Could this have anything to do with the mystery of the missing tiara?

Most of the other party guests had drifted away after the excitement had passed. But a few were still hanging around the table.

"Have you ever seen the ghost yourself, Jackson?" one of them asked.

Jackson smiled, seeming to snap out of his thoughts. "Oh, no," he replied. "Not really. There have been times when I thought I *felt* something, a certain presence if you will, but of course who can say . . ."

"Come on," I said, tugging at Ned's sleeve.

Soon my friends and I were huddled in a private spot in the corner of the room. "This is getting weird," Bess declared.

"Do you think that the thief planted that mask?" Ned asked.

I pursed my lips. "Maybe," I said. "If Jackson didn't do it—and I don't think he did—why would anyone else pull such a mean trick? Everyone is here to support Jackson. The thief could be trying to distract us from finding out exactly who he is."

"Seems kind of a bizarre way to do it," Bess said.

"I know." I wondered if we were wasting time talking about this. What if the mask had been planted by some random troublemaker or jokester with no connection to the crime? We could spend half the night investigating it and be no closer to finding the thief. "We need George," I said. "She's spent quite a bit of time up in Lisette's bedroom tonight. Maybe she noticed whether that mask was there earlier, or when it might have disappeared. That could give us some kind of clue."

Bess nodded. "She might even have a picture of it in her camera."

"Should we head upstairs?" Ned asked.

I started to nod. But just as we were heading toward the stairs, I heard a burst of muffled laughter. It seemed to be coming from somewhere down the hall. "Hold on," I said. "Maybe she's down there."

"It's worth a look," Bess agreed.

Soon we found ourselves in a short hallway. Halfway down the hallway was a door, which was ajar. Voices were coming from behind it.

Pushing the door open farther, I saw a small, cozy room that appeared to be both a den and an office. The voices turned out to belong to Maureen Ardmore and a couple of her friends. They were lounging on a pair of leather couches, shoes off and drinks in their hands. There was a desk with a computer against one wall, and a few chairs clustered near a small fireplace on the facing wall. Thick velvet curtains hung over the windows, and a dusty old Oriental rug covered the wooden floorboards.

Maureen was talking as we entered. ". . . and whenever crazy old Uncle Jackson finally comes to his senses and sells this rotten old place, Mom says the first thing we can do is get new cars for both of us, and I—" She cut herself off abruptly as she spotted me standing there. "Oh. Hello. Can I help you?"

"Hi, Maureen. It's me, Nancy. Nancy Drew?"

She blinked lazily at me. "Oh, right. I know you." She stretched and sat up, yanking down the hem of her slinky gold gown over her long, slim legs. Seeing Ned come in behind me and Bess, she tilted her head and shot him a smile. "How's it going?"

Her friends just sipped their drinks and stared at us wordlessly. One of them was a guy named Steve who worked at one of the local pizza places, and the other was a short, olive-skinned girl I didn't know, though I'd seen her around town.

"Sorry to interrupt," I said. "We were just looking for someone. Um, also, there was a bit of commotion out front just now. Have you guys seen or heard anything odd tonight?"

Maureen tossed her head and laughed. Her thick, chestnut hair flopped over her face, and she pushed it back impatiently. "What do you think, guys?" she asked her friends playfully. "Have we seen anything odd tonight?"

"Depends on your definition of odd," the other girl drawled.

"Yeah." Maureen stood up and stretched, then grabbed the magenta and gold beaded mask lying on the coffee table and snapped it on. "I guess it does. What's your definition of the word odd, Nancy Drew?"

"Never mind." I could see we weren't going to get very far here. I should have known. Maureen has never taken much of anything seriously, from school

to part-time jobs to her endless series of boyfriends—
she goes through them almost as quickly as Deirdre
does.

"Let's check upstairs for George," Bess murmured
in my ear as Maureen and her friends headed for the
door.

I nodded, and we fell in step behind Maureen
and company as they wandered out toward the main
room, still talking and laughing together. Ned and
Bess started up the steps right away, but I lingered
back a little while, watching as Maureen and her
friends stepped out into the party. The mysterious
Derek was standing near the entryway when they
came in. He spotted Maureen immediately and his
eyes lit up. Soon he was at her side and they were
talking. I noticed the way he was touching her arm
and smiling at her. Interesting . . .

"Coming, Nancy?" Bess called from halfway up
the stairs.

"Coming." I turned away from the party and hurried back to join my friends. Ned was standing on
the first landing, peering out a small, diamond-shaped
window with green and white panes.

"Hey," he said. "There's someone outside—down
there, see? Kind of lurking around by the solarium."

Bess leaned down to look through one of the
white panes. "I think it's George!" she exclaimed.

We raced back downstairs and reached the back door just as George let herself in. She was holding her camera in one hand and her skirt with the other. Her mask was dangling from its string around her neck.

"What are you guys doing back here?" she asked, pushing the door shut behind her.

"I have a better question. Where have *you* been?" Bess demanded. "We've been looking all over."

George shrugged. "Just taking a peek into the solarium." She sounded a bit defensive. "And no, I didn't go inside. I promised I wouldn't, remember?"

"That's good. But listen, we have to tell you something." I filled her in on the mystery.

"Wow," George said when I'd finished. She grinned. "So Deirdre really stepped in it this time, huh?"

"That's not nice," Bess chided. "She came to us for help."

"She went to *Nancy* for help," George corrected. "And only because she knew Nancy was her only chance of wriggling out of this without getting in trouble."

Ned chuckled. "True. But this isn't only about Deirdre," he pointed out. "That tiara is not only worth a lot of money, but it's a valuable historical and family heirloom. It would be terrible to have it fall into the hands of a thief."

"Good point." George nodded thoughtfully. "So who are our suspects so far?"

"We only have one," Bess said. "Derek."

George's eyes narrowed. "I *knew* that guy was up to no good!"

"Not so fast," I said. "I'm not sure he could've done it. Besides, there's someone else we should add to the list: Maureen Ardmore."

"Maureen?" Ned turned to me in surprise. "Why her?"

"Didn't you hear what she was saying when we walked in on her just now?" I tapped my foot on the linoleum floor of the hallway, trying to remember exactly what I'd overheard. "It kind of sounded like she's expecting to strike it rich if Jackson sells this house. And it also kind of sounded like she thought that might happen sometime soon."

Bess bit her lip. "Wow," she said. "I always knew Maureen was kind of spoiled. And she likes to goof around, so I can almost see her pulling a stunt like dropping that mask in the punch bowl. She and her friends probably could've planted it there and scooted back to the room in time for us to find them. But what would make her steal Deirdre's tiara?"

"I think I know." Ned looked grim. "Nancy and I heard Maureen's mother, Patricia, arguing with Jackson earlier. What if the two of them are conspiring to pressure Jackson into selling before he can apply to the Antique Homes Registry? A high-profile theft and a bunch of ghostly annoyances might do the trick, especially if they ruined the fund-raiser in the process."

By now George was starting to look intrigued. "Okay, so why were you wasting time looking for me instead of investigating all this?" she asked. "I mean, I know I'm brilliant and all, but . . ."

"We were hoping you might have noticed that white mask upstairs earlier," I said. "It should have been hanging on the wall with a bunch of others."

George shrugged. "Yeah, there are masks all over that one wall upstairs. I didn't look at them that carefully, though."

"Did you get any photos of them?" Ned asked.

"Let me check." George leaned back against the wall and quickly scrolled through the snapshots stored on her camera. "Yeah, here we go."

She held out the camera and I peered at the little screen. "There it is," I said, spotting the distinctive white mask immediately. It had held a place of honor right in the middle of the display. "What time did you take this picture?"

George pulled back the camera and peered at it. "About half an hour ago," she said. "Why? What difference does it make?"

"I'm not sure." I sighed. "I guess it just means that someone must have taken it since the time you were last up there."

George was looking down at the camera viewer again. "Maybe it was the ghost," she said. "Do you guys want to see that foggy mirror picture again?"

I ignored the question, turning to Bess and Ned. "I don't know if this mask thing means anything. But we can't ignore it, just in case. Whoever took that mask must have been upstairs within the past half hour. Can you two go circulate and see if you can find out who might have left the main rooms lately and who definitely hasn't? At least that might give us somewhere to start."

"You got it," Ned said, and Bess nodded.

"Thanks." I knew they would be the perfect ones for the job. Both of them are good at talking to people and careful enough not to raise any suspicions.

"So what are we going to do in the meantime?" George asked as the other two hurried off toward the main rooms.

"I want to check out Lisette's bedroom for myself," I said. "Maybe there are some clues up there. You can come with me."

"Oh." George sounded underwhelmed by the plan. "Actually, I have a better idea. While you do that, why don't I go outside and take a look around? I noticed there's an outside stairway to the second floor—some kind of fire escape, I guess. I can check for footprints at the bottom of it in case the thief escaped that way."

"An outside stairway? Really?" I was surprised and intrigued. "Where is it? I never noticed anything like that."

"You can't really see it from the street," George said. "It's hidden behind the side porch."

"Interesting. Maybe I'll go take a look at that first." I was already heading for the door.

"No, wait." George grabbed my arm. "I just had another idea."

"What is it?" I stopped and turned to face her.

"I just thought of one more suspect you should add to the list," George said. "Jackson Ayers."

"Jackson?" I repeated.

"Think about it," George said. "That tiara belonged to his grandmother, and anyone can see that Jackson is totally attached to all his old heirlooms and stuff. It must be killing him that he had to sell such an important piece. Maybe he saw this as a way to get back something that he never really wanted to lose in the first place."

"That makes some sense," I agreed thoughtfully.

George grabbed me by the arm. "Of course it does, Nancy!" she insisted, her eyes glittering with urgency. "It makes perfect sense. You should definitely go question Jackson—right away!"

7

Sightings

I was a little surprised by her passion. George often comes up with good ideas and theories during cases, but she's not usually quite so emphatic about them. Still, I had to admit she had a good point. Jackson did have a pretty strong motive for snatching that tiara.

"Maybe you're right," I said. "Come to think of it, he said something sort of funny to Patricia earlier."

"Funny ha-ha, or funny suspicious?" George asked.

"Suspicious." I chewed my lip, trying to remember exactly what he'd said. "It was something about how after tonight, none of them would have to worry about money anymore. At the time I assumed he was referring to the fund-raiser, but maybe there was more to it than that." I took a step toward the main rooms. "I think maybe I will go have a chat with him."

"Great." George grinned at me. "I'll go take a look outside and meet up with you in a few."

We parted ways, and I headed back to the party area. When I entered, I spotted Jackson right away. He was standing near the fireplace talking with Patricia and Maureen.

A-ha! I thought. Three birds with one stone!

But I'd barely taken three steps when I noticed Deirdre and Adam making a beeline for me. "Nancy!" Deirdre called out. "There you are." She grabbed me and hustled me back out to the relative privacy of the stairwell. Adam followed. "So what's happening?" Deirdre demanded. "Did you figure out who took the tiara?"

"I'm working on it, Deirdre," I said, trying to sound patient. "It's not going to happen instantly, especially since nobody is supposed to know about this. But don't worry, we're making progress."

Deirdre rolled her eyes and blew out an impatient sigh. "I don't even know why I bothered to tell you about this," she complained.

Beside her, Adam cleared his throat. "Hey, I just thought of something," he said uncertainly. "Um, I don't know if it's important or not, but I guess it might be."

"What is it?" I asked, though considering his earlier vague "theory" I didn't have much hope.

"When Deirdre went to the bathroom, I went outside, remember?" he said. "While I was out on the porch, something dripped on my shoulder from overhead."

"Ew!" Deirdre looked horrified.

"Don't worry, it was just water," Adam told her quickly. "I guess it was rain dripping from the gutters or something." He turned back to me. "Anyway, I headed inside to the kitchen to see if I could find a towel. On my way there, I saw someone running through the solarium. I only noticed because I'd heard it was off-limits." He shrugged. "But I just realized that must have been right around the same time as the theft. Do you think it might mean something?"

If Adam has his details right, this was huge! I couldn't believe he hadn't mentioned it until now.

Seeming to guess at least some of what I was thinking, Adam smiled apologetically. "I'm really sorry I didn't remember sooner." He reached over and took Deirdre by the arm. "I guess I just forgot everything when Deirdre told me what happened. I was so worried about whether she was okay. And then when I realized what was up with the tiara, I couldn't stop thinking about how furious my father would be." He shot a glance at Mr. Fielding, who was chatting with some people near the catering table.

"It's okay," I told Adam. "But listen, I need you

to think back and tell me exactly what you saw. Which way was the person going? Was it a man or a woman?"

"All I saw was a figure rushing through the middle of the solarium heading for the outside door on the west side," Adam said. "I didn't get a good enough look to tell whether it was a man or a woman. Whoever it was definitely looked like they were on the short side—a good bit shorter than me, and fairly slender." He scrunched up his face thoughtfully. "It could have been a woman, or maybe a smallish man. I'm really not sure."

I nodded. Short and slight, I thought. That definitely eliminates Mr. Fielding, who's neither. But it could still fit Patricia, Maureen, or Jackson. Possibly even Derek, though if Adam has the timing right it couldn't be him for other reasons.

"Well, what are you waiting for, Nancy?" Deirdre said. "Adam just practically solved the mystery for you—what more do you want? You should go out to that door he mentioned and look for footprints or something. Isn't that what detectives are supposed to do?"

"Yes," I said calmly. "That's exactly what we do."

"Except that ghosts don't leave footprints, remember?" Adam put in. "What if this all has something to do with that ghost?"

Deirdre rolled her eyes so hard I was afraid they'd pop out of her head. "You *are* kidding, right?" she said. "That was no ghost that grabbed me in the bathroom. It was a human. A greedy, obnoxious one, but still—definitely human."

Adam smiled weakly. "Oh, um, of course I was kidding. I don't believe in ghosts either." Suddenly his smile disappeared. "Uh-oh," he muttered. "Here comes that jerk."

Glancing over, I saw Derek wandering in our general direction, though he didn't appear to have spotted us yet. It was only a matter of time, though—Deirdre wasn't exactly inconspicuous, especially in that dress. I winced, hoping I wasn't about to witness *Clash of the Overly Macho Men, Part Three.*

Luckily Adam didn't seem any more eager for a rerun than I was. "Come on," he said, dragging Deirdre off in the opposite direction. "Let's go get some more punch or something."

"Fine, whatever." Deirdre allowed herself to be pulled away. She glanced at me over her shoulder with a frown. "But hurry up! We don't have much time."

Once they had disappeared into the crowd, I ducked back into the stairwell, not wanting Derek to spot me. He seemed willing to flirt with any girl he saw, and I just didn't have the time.

I still wanted to talk to Jackson, but after Adam's

story, I decided I'd better take a look outside first. If there were any footprints or other clues to be found, I wanted to get to them before a caterer dragging a trash bag or a neighbor's wandering dog accidentally destroyed them.

Spinning around, I hurried toward the door just past the den. The solarium door would be just around the corner from there. But before I could get there, the door burst open and George raced in, moving so fast that she almost crashed into me.

"Nancy!" she cried, wheezing for breath. "There you are!"

Her face was bright red and her eyes were wide and excited. My heart jumped—had she cracked the case?

"What is it?" I demanded. "Did you find something? A clue?"

"What? No." George shook her head so violently that the mask perched atop of it almost flew off. "But check this out—I finally got a shot of that ghost!"

8

Facts and Figures

My shoulders slumped with disappointment as George pushed her camera in front of me. The picture in the viewer showed a rather fuzzy shot of one of the mansion's upstairs windows. A shadowy, blobby, and vaguely humanoid figure was standing there with one arm outstretched.

"See?" George said. "I told you guys not to laugh!" She bounded past me, heading for the stairs. "I'm going to see if it's still up there!"

I sighed, not bothering to try to stop her. For one thing, I knew it wouldn't do any good. Besides, I figured if her photo had just captured evidence of someone of the nonghostly variety lurking around upstairs where they didn't belong, it might turn out to have something to do with the case. It wasn't as if I had a whole lot of other solid leads at the moment.

"Nancy?" Bess's voice interrupted my thoughts. I turned to see her walking toward me from the direction of the party. "Was that George I just saw racing up the steps four at a time? What's going on?"

"You don't want to know," I said. But I filled her in anyway.

She shook her head. "That's our George."

"What about you? Have you and Ned found out anything interesting?"

"Not much," she admitted. "Ned's still out there—Mr. Geffington cornered him and is talking his ear off about the stock market or something." She shrugged. "It turns out it's not easy to confirm alibis for people when you can't tell them why you need to know."

I smiled sympathetically. "Just give me what you've got."

"Well, as we already know, Derek was around in my plain sight during the robbery." Bess grimaced slightly at the thought. "But nobody seems to have seen him during the blackout, and it's only off and on afterward. The only other person whose whereabouts at the time of the robbery I've been able to verify is Maureen Ardmore. She was dancing at the time—apparently rather wildly, since more than one person mentioned it."

"Nothing on the others?"

"Not yet. Jackson, Patricia, Mr. Fielding . . . I haven't been able to pin down where they were during the robbery, the blackout, or the mask incident."

I nodded thoughtfully. "Thanks for trying. By the way, I almost forgot—I ran into Deirdre and Adam, and Adam gave me another lead." I told her about the mysterious figure in the solarium.

"Are we sure it wasn't George?" Bess asked skeptically. "She was missing during that time period, wasn't she?"

"Good point. I didn't think of that," I admitted. "She claims she hasn't gone in there, but it couldn't hurt to ask one more time."

"Right." Bess tapped her chin with one finger, looking thoughtful. "While we're on the subject, are you sure Adam was telling the truth about the figure being in the solarium? What if he's covering up for his father?"

"That's what I'm starting to wonder too," I said. "After all, what better way to throw us off the scent than to make us think the thief is short and slim? That's pretty much the opposite of Mr. Fielding."

"True. Then again, it's hard to imagine Mr. Fielding slipping in and out of the powder room fast enough that Deirdre couldn't get a good look at him. That place isn't exactly roomy. Wouldn't Deirdre have noticed if she'd been grabbed by someone that, er, large?"

"You're probably right," I said. "But what if Mr. Fielding convinced Adam to steal the tiara for him? Then it would still make sense for Adam to try to throw us off with that story about the figure in the solarium." I shrugged. "After all, who better to set up something like that? He would know exactly when Deirdre would be off by herself."

"You're right!" Bess's blue eyes widened. "Is there any way to double-check Adam's story?"

"Well, I was just going to go look for footprints out where he said. He made a funny comment about how ghosts don't leave footprints right after he told me the solarium story, almost as if he realized too late that his story didn't—oh! I know," I interrupted myself. "He also said he went into the kitchen for a towel right around the time of the theft. That should be easy enough to confirm—there's been catering staff in and out of there all night."

"I'll go check it out if you want," Bess offered.

"Great! Then I can take a look around for those footprints."

Bess disappeared down the hallway to the kitchen. I started toward the back door, but once again I heard a voice calling behind me.

This time, unfortunately, it was Deirdre. "What

are you doing just standing around?" she demanded shrilly, her expression bordering on hysteria. "You're supposed to be finding that tiara!"

I debated whether to remind her that we'd just discussed this not ten minutes earlier. Deciding it wouldn't do any good, I pasted what I hoped was a comforting smile on my face.

"Don't worry, Deirdre," I said. "We're making progress. You just need to be patient a little bit longer so we can—"

"I don't have time to be patient!" she shrieked, clearly ready to panic. "This party will be over in like an hour! What am I supposed to do then?" She clutched at her hair. Now I *knew* she was panicking. That was the only way she'd risk damaging her hairdresser's hours of hard work. "Maybe Adam is right— I should start trying to pull that ransom together just in case. If I explain things to my parents, they'll find a way to get the cash on short notice." She broke off in a sob.

"That won't be necessary," I told her firmly. I stepped over and grabbed her by both shoulders, forcing her to face me. "Listen to me, Deirdre. Don't do anything drastic, okay? Just give me a little more time. I can solve this if you just give me the chance."

Deirdre blinked at me with surprise. "Why should I believe that?"

"Because we're getting closer to the thief, I can tell." Seeing that she still looked doubtful, I added, "I'm going outside right now to look for footprints."

"Okay." Deirdre didn't sound too impressed with that plan. But at least the frantic look was leaving her eyes. "But hurry up, okay? I guess I'd better go find Adam and let him know you're actually, you know, doing stuff or whatever. I think he's starting to freak out a little."

She hurried off, and I sighed with relief. Then I turned and headed for the back door. Miraculously nothing came along to stop me this time, and I let myself outside.

The night air was still cool and damp, and my high-heeled shoes sank into the yielding ground as soon as I stepped off the gravel path. A light breeze ruffled the feathers on the mask I was clutching in my hand, and loose strands of my hair fluttered around my cheeks.

I belatedly realized that a flashlight would be helpful in this investigation, but I didn't want to take the time to go back inside and look for one. There was just barely enough light seeping out through the windows to see.

Carefully tiptoeing my way across the damp grass, I rounded the back corner of the house. Now the solarium lay before me, its skeletal metal framework seeming to clutch for dear life on to the solid brick walls of the house. I squinted into the dark interior, trying to imagine what the solarium must have been like in its prime. A glow emanated from the back interior wall, outlining the tall, bowed forms of the remaining palms. It was really kind of creepy.

I turned away, casting my gaze downward. One thing was for sure—if anyone had been back here tonight, the soft, rain-soaked ground would show the evidence. I walked slowly along the long back wall of the solarium, staying well out in the grass to avoid puncturing any footprints with those annoying high heels Bess had insisted I wear.

I paused near the first of three sets of French doors along the solarium, peering carefully at the ground in front of them. There were a couple of flat stepping stones set into the dirt path leading up to the threshold. The stones were fairly small and rough, and not very easy to see in the dim light. Could someone pass from the yard into the solarium using the stones so as not to leave a print? I wasn't sure.

I moved on to the next set of doors. Gathering up my skirt as best I could, I stepped forward carefully, bending down to squint at the dirt-and-stone path.

Is that something? I wondered, leaning even farther forward as I spotted a tiny rough spot in the dirt.

If someone was stepping on this stone and slipped to the side just a little, then maybe . . .

I was so engrossed in what I was doing that it wasn't until I heard a funny little hissing noise nearby that I noticed a cloying floral scent wrapping its way around my nostrils. I wriggled my nose, glancing up in confusion at the solarium right in front of me. I gasped as I saw a shadowy, indistinct figure reflected in the glass wall.

"Who—?" I blurted out, starting to turn around.

But it was too late. I felt a hard shove on my back. My feet slipped out from under me and I went flying headfirst into the glass-and-steel solarium wall.

9

Light Show

My head struck the glass with a ringing thud, and I slumped to the ground. For a moment I felt like one of those cartoon characters with stars spinning around their heads. My only coherent thought was that the old solarium wall sure felt a lot sturdier than it looked.

From behind me, I was vaguely aware of footsteps running away across the spacious backyard. But I was far too dazed to turn and look.

By the time I got my wits about me, it was too late. My attacker had disappeared. I stared off across the yard, which was lost in a shadowy mass of shrubs and trees. I climbed to my feet slowly, wincing both at my throbbing head and the muddy stains on my rented dress.

Ignoring both problems for the time being, I looked around. My attacker had left a few footprints behind, but they were too smudged to tell much beyond the fact that they'd been made by men's dress shoes. That faint flowery scent was still lingering in the damp air. I sniffed, trying to place it. It seemed familiar somehow. . . .

"Magnolia," I whispered as the answer clicked into my aching head. Hannah had some magnolia-scented powder that she liked to use on special occasions— that was where I'd smelled it before.

Interesting, I thought, glancing back at the gloomy solarium, behind whose thick glass walls tender southern magnolias had once bloomed.

All my body parts still seemed to be functioning, and even the pain in my head was already fading, though I was sure I'd have a lovely bruise the next day. My friends always said I was hardheaded. . . .

I took a few steps into the yard, trying to see if the attacker had left more footprints. But as soon as I got a few dozen feet out from the house, it was too dark to see much. Chasing down the guy wasn't looking to be a useful option.

Instead I turned and hurried back around the corner of the house to the side doors. At least there was a chance I could see who was missing from the party.

I clambered up onto the porch, slipping a little in

my damp shoes. The door flew open as I was quickly brushing the worst of the dirt and wet off my skirt.

"Nancy!" Deirdre stood framed in the doorway with Adam behind her. "What did that poor dress ever do to you? You're a mess!"

Adam pushed past her and hurried to my side. "What happened?" he asked with concern. "Did you fall? Are you hurt?"

"I'll be okay. Just took a spill on the wet grass," I fibbed.

He was staring at my forehead. "What's that big red spot? Did you bump your head?"

"Maybe a little," I said weakly, glancing longingly past him into the house. "Listen, I'll be fine. I need to get inside and—"

"Does all this have something to do with that stolen tiara?" Adam asked, sounding more concerned than ever. "If you're putting yourself at risk, it's not worth it. Deirdre and I have already figured out a way to get part of the ransom money, so if you want to give up . . ."

Deirdre looked horrified. "Are you crazy?" she exclaimed at Adam. "I'm not handing over *any* money to some jerky low-life thief unless I have no other choice! I keep telling you Nancy is working on this. And you heard her—she's fine."

"Thanks for the vote of confidence, Deirdre," I said dryly. "Now if you two will excuse me . . ."

I finally managed to go around them and head inside. But I didn't bother to hurry as I headed down the hall toward the front of the house. The moment had passed. In the time I'd wasted talking to Deirdre and Adam, my attacker could have circled back around and reentered the party through a different door.

Ned was chatting with someone when I came into the main room, but he excused himself and hurried over as soon as he saw me. "What happened to you?" he asked, pulling off his mask and tucking it in his jacket pocket.

I pulled him out into the hall by the stairs and then told him the whole story. "I was hoping to get back in here in time to see who might be mysteriously absent," I finished. "But I ran into Deirdre on the way in. Bad luck."

His forehead creased with worry. "How hard did you hit your head?" he asked, reaching out and gingerly touching the red spot on my temple. "Dr. Milner is here tonight—maybe you should ask her to take a look. Or at least sit down and rest for a few minutes."

I brushed his hand away. "I'm fine," I insisted. "Anyway, there's no time for that. This proves that the thief is still hanging around. And we're obviously making him nervous. That must mean we're getting closer."

"Maybe." Ned sounded dubious. "But it sure doesn't *feel* like we're any closer."

I absently rubbed at a smudge on my skirt. "We must be missing something," I said, thinking hard. "We have plenty of suspects, but none of them seems quite right. Some of them couldn't have done it given the timing—"

"Derek, because he was with Bess. And Maureen, because all those people saw her dancing." Ned supplied with a nod.

"Right. And Mr. Fielding probably couldn't have been the one who grabbed the tiara because Deirdre would have noticed his size. But that doesn't mean he isn't working with Adam. Although come to think of it, that doesn't quite work either." I chewed on my lower lip. "I'm sure it wasn't Mr. Fielding who pushed me just now."

"Doesn't seem like his style," Ned said.

"Not just that. I don't think he could've run off that quickly afterward." I shrugged. "But it couldn't have been Adam that pushed me either. He was with Deirdre when I ran into her on my way in. There wasn't enough time for him to circle back around that fast."

"So the Fieldings are out, and Maureen is out, and probably Derek," Ned said. "Who's left?"

"Maureen could still be involved," I said. "She

obviously wasn't the one who grabbed the tiara, but she could be working with her mother, or Jackson, or maybe somebody else if she . . . what?"

I noticed Ned staring off over my shoulder, tilting his head to one side. "Do you hear that?" he asked.

I turned and looked down the hall leading back to the kitchen. Now that we'd stopped talking, I could hear what Ned's sharp ears had already picked up—a commotion of exclamations and chatter from the back of the house.

"I hope the kitchen's not on fire or something," Ned said. "That's the last thing Jackson needs right now."

"Let's go see." I was already hurrying off to look.

We soon realized the noise wasn't actually coming from the kitchen. It was coming from the nearby hallway adjoining the solarium. A small crowd was gathered there. Some people were huddled back against the wall, while others were standing with their faces pressed to the windows and French doors. All of them were staring into the darkened solarium.

I soon saw why. Green, gold, and purple lights were dancing about among the shadowy palms like enormous fireflies.

Ned let out a low whistle. "Weird," he said.

"It's Mardi Gras colors, get it?" someone cried out.

A woman from my volunteer group shrieked with mock fear. "It's Lisette! She's after us!"

"Or maybe she just wants to taste the gumbo they're serving tonight," the mayor's teenage daughter commented.

There were nervous titters of laughter from the other observers. I stepped toward the closest set of doors, my heart pounding. I knew it wasn't a ghost making those lights, Lisette or otherwise. And whoever was doing it was probably inside right now . . .

Before I could reach the doors, I spotted Jackson hurrying down the hall toward us. "What's going on?" he cried out. "Is there a—oh!"

He stopped and stared into the solarium. All the color drained from his face as stared at the dancing multicolored lights.

I had stopped too, knowing that Jackson wouldn't let me into the solarium. "Any idea who could be doing that?" I asked him instead. "It's not part of the party plans, is it?"

He was still staring in at the lights. "No," he said slowly. "That is, *I* certainly didn't plan it." He rubbed his face with a shaking hand and shook his head. "I just hope this doesn't mean Lisette is . . ." The last sentence was muttered under his breath, and faded away too quickly to catch the end. I exchanged a glance with Ned, wondering if he'd heard it too.

"They're gone!" someone cried, pointing.

Glancing back into the solarium, I saw that it was true. The lights had winked out.

The crowd started murmuring and exclaiming all over again. Jackson was already pleading for calm and trying to herd everyone back out to the party. I debated hanging around and trying to sneak into the solarium after they'd all left, but decided against it. After all, the thief—if that's who had done it—surely wasn't stupid enough to hang around in there now that the show was over.

"Come on," I said, grabbing Ned by the arm.

We headed back out to the stairwell, which was still deserted. "So what was that all about?" he asked.

"This is weird," I said, staring down at the floor-boards as I paced back and forth in front of the bottom step. "Someone must have gone to a lot of trouble to set up that little spectacle in the solarium. Why bother?"

"Not necessarily," Ned said. "It was hard to see much through that foggy old glass. But it kind of looked to me like just a few flashlights with colored fabric or cellophane or something over the end. All someone had to do was sneak in there and wave them around a little, and voila! Ghostly Mardi Gras light show."

I stopped and looked at him, impressed with his

quick thinking. "Really?" I said. "Hmm. So almost anybody on our suspect list could've managed it."

"Anybody except Jackson. He came in before the lights stopped."

I nodded, thinking back to make sure none of our other potential thieves had been among the watching crowd. "I guess it's like I was saying before," I said. "Whoever took that tiara knows we're after him, and he's trying to distract us or throw us off the scent with all this ghost business. The mask in the punch bowl, those lights just now, that picture George took . . ."

"What picture?" Ned asked. "You're not talking about that mirror smudge, are you?"

I shook my head. "Different picture. She was outside looking around and caught some shot of a ghostly-looking figure in an upstairs window," I said. "She showed it to me right before I—"

Suddenly Ned lunged forward. "Nancy, look out!"

I glanced up to see something flying down out of the darkness, coming straight at me.

10

Fan Mail

I ducked just in time. The object landed with a clatter and skidded off across the polished wooden floor. "Are you okay?" Ned cried.

As soon as I nodded, he took off, bounding up the steps three at a time. I started up after him, but after almost tripping over my skirt on the first step, I thought better of it. I wasn't dressed for running.

"Be careful!" I called after Ned. Up above, I heard a rush of footsteps as whoever was up there ran away down the upstairs hall.

Then I turned to look for the thing that had been thrown at me. It only took a moment to find it in a dark corner behind the stairs. It was a fan—the kind that folds up. I unfurled it carefully. It was gorgeous and old-fashioned, red and gold with black lace edges.

I wasn't sure, but I thought I'd seen this very same fan in one of George's photos of Lisette's bedroom. It had been hanging on the wall near the dresser mirror.

As the last few folds of the fan opened up, something white fluttered out and fell to the floor. I picked it up and unfolded it. Stepping over to the powder room door, which was ajar, I flipped on the light so I could see better.

It was a typed note:

```
Stay out of family business,
nosy Nancy. U shouldn't stick ur
nose where it doesn't belong or
someone will get hurt.
```

"Hey! What's a beautiful girl like you doing out here all alone?" Derek strolled in from the main room just as I finished scanning the note. "Need some company, sweetheart?"

I quickly tucked both note and fan into my bag. "No thanks," I said, doing my best to hide my irritation at his untimely arrival. "I was just, uh, using the restroom." I reached over and flicked off the bathroom light.

"Powdering your pretty little nose, eh?" He stepped a little closer, leering at me in the dim hallway light. "Well, it worked. You look fantastic."

I bit back an annoyed retort, realizing that his unwelcome appearance had served a purpose after all. If I'd still entertained any lingering thoughts that Derek could be the culprit, this was another strike against that idea. Not only couldn't he have been the original thief, but he also definitely *hadn't* been the one who'd thrown that fan at me. There hadn't been time for him to run away, make it down the fire escape, and come back inside through the front door and back to the stairway—especially since he wasn't even the least bit breathless.

All this crossed my mind in an instant. Meanwhile Derek was still gazing at me with his smug grin. "It's Nelly, right?" he said. "We met outside."

"It's Nancy, actually," I corrected him. I didn't bother to correct the fact that we hadn't technically met at all, since he'd been too busy drooling over Deirdre to introduce himself to anyone else.

"Nancy," he repeated. "Pretty name for a pretty girl."

I was still rolling my eyes at the cheesy line when Ned came thumping back down the stairs. He spotted Derek right away and frowned.

"Back off, buddy," he said briskly. "Nancy is with me." As Derek opened his mouth to respond, Ned added, "And no, I didn't make that decision for her, so don't even bother."

Snapping his mouth shut, Derek shrugged. "Whatever, dude." He shoved his hands in his pockets and slouched off, disappearing a moment later into the main room.

"Nice work," I told him with a grin. "You should give Adam some lessons."

"Never mind that." Ned sighed. "Whoever just tried to give you another bump on the head got away again. Must've ducked out a window or down the fire escape before I could catch up."

"Was there anybody upstairs at all?" I asked.

"Not that I found. I took a quick look around once I realized I'd lost him, just in case he was hiding somewhere."

I nodded. "I guess I should've run out to see if anyone turned up on the fire escape. But I was distracted by this."

I showed him the fan and the note. Ned read it over several times, rubbing his chin with one hand.

"Looks like this was typed up on a computer," he said. "And whoever wrote it obviously knows your name."

I dug into my purse again. This time I pulled out Deirdre's ransom note. Holding it up beside the new note, I compared them.

"Same font," I said. "And look—both of them use

u and *ur* for *you* and *your*. The same person must have typed them."

Ned looked up at me, an idea already on his lips. "That ransom note could've been printed up any-time . . ."

". . . but the new one must have been done within the past hour or so," I finished for him. "That means the computer that was used to type this is either right here in the house or very close by."

"Could be a laptop in someone's car," he suggested.

"Maybe, but then how would they print it out?" I carefully folded up the notes and stuck them back in my purse. "Let's go take a look at that computer in the den."

Just then Bess and George hurried in from the back hallway. "Just the people we were looking for!" Bess said when she spotted us.

"Hey, you found the mighty ghost hunter," Ned joked. "Got a shot of Bigfoot yet, George? Maybe the Loch Ness monster swimming in a bathtub?"

George made a face. "You're hysterical."

"Did you find out anything in the kitchen?" I asked Bess, recalling her earlier errand.

"Yes and no," she said. "The catering staff definitely remembered seeing Adam after I described him." She smiled. "A couple of them were making fun of his dorky mask. The trouble is, they weren't sure exactly when he was there—they thought they'd seen him a couple of times, but they were way too busy to have noted the time."

"Well, at least that makes his story a little more credible," I said. "I guess we can give him the benefit of the doubt for now, especially since we've pretty much ruled out the father-and-son theory anyway." I quickly updated her and George about everything Ned and I had discussed and experienced since seeing them last. They were both concerned to hear of my way-too-close encounter with the wall outside, and George was fascinated when I described the dancing colored lights we'd seen in the solarium.

"That pretty much matches some of the ghost stories I found online," she said. "I wish I'd been there to get a picture."

On our way to the little office, I showed them both the new note and explained our mission.

"No problem," George said confidently as we stepped into the deserted room. "If this note was typed up on that computer, I'll be able to pull it up—no matter how tricky someone tried to be in deleting or hiding it."

Ned was already over at the desk. "That won't be necessary," he said, leaning down for a better look at the computer screen. "Check it out."

I hurried over to join him. The computer was on, and the message from my note was still on the screen.

"Wow," Bess said. "Looks like someone was in a hurry."

George pushed the rest of us aside and sat down. "Let's see if I can find that ransom note on here too."

She worked her computer magic and within minutes the text of Deirdre's note was flickering out at us from the screen. I stared at it.

"This certainly seems to point toward Jackson or his family members," I said slowly, thinking out loud. "But then again, anyone could have sneaked in here and printed out those notes."

"Deirdre would probably insist on you dusting the keyboard for fingerprints," George said, spinning around in the desk chair to face the rest of us.

I chuckled. "Not a bad idea," I said. "Although even if you hadn't already touched the keyboard and ruined the evidence, I doubt the thief would be that careless."

"Plus if you found Jackson's prints, or Patricia's or Maureen's, it wouldn't really tell you anything, since they all have other reasons to use that computer," Ned added.

"That's true." I bit my lip and stared at the screen. "But you know, the more we look into this, the more Jackson himself seems like the prime suspect."

"Jackson?" Bess wrinkled her nose. "It's hard to

imagine him mugging Deirdre like that."

"I know. I can't picture him shoving me into that glass wall either, or being fast and agile enough to escape from Ned just now." I sighed. "But think about it. He certainly seems to be the romantic type when it comes to his family history, and he's definitely attached to this old house. Plus he's familiar with all the ghost stories. Maybe he does regret selling that tiara enough to try to steal it back. He might have hired some thug . . ."

"Like Derek!" George spoke up eagerly. "He totally seems like the thug type."

"It couldn't have been Derek," Bess reminded her. "He was with me during the robbery, remember?"

"Plus he turned up at the same time Ned was chasing the fan thrower just now." I turned and wandered across the room, still turning over all the clues in my head. "So not Derek. But there are lots of people here tonight; maybe one of them is desperate for cash and agreed to help out. Or maybe his accomplice is Patricia or Maureen, or both—they both seem way too interested in money."

"So what do we do now? Question Patricia and Maureen?" Ned asked.

"Not quite yet," I replied. "Might as well go to the source. I think we're long overdue for a little chat with Jackson."

11

Suspect Small Talk

We decided that I would talk to Jackson alone while my friends kept sniffing around for more clues. I headed back into the main room and spotted him over by the fireplace chatting with Harold Safer.

Pasting a smile on my face, I grabbed a glass of punch and headed over. I arrived just as Mr. Safer wandered off.

"Well hello, Nancy," Jackson greeted me. "I hope you're having a nice time."

"Oh, I am." I waved a hand at the crowded room. "I think everyone here is having fun. You've had a terrific turnout tonight."

"Yes, it's very gratifying," Jackson said softly, glancing around. "It's lovely to know that so many people are willing to help—that I'm not just a foolish old man to be so fond of this old place."

I took a sip of my drink. "Everyone seems to be enjoying the Mardi Gras atmosphere a lot, too. The decorations, the food, the little ghostly touches . . ." Seeing him frown slightly, I quickly added, "I'm sorry—did I say something wrong?"

"No, no, it's not you, dear." He patted me on the arm. "I'm just so worried. People are still talking about everything that's gone wrong tonight: that mask ending up in the punch, the lights in the solarium, and of course that terrible blackout."

"I see," I said. He certainly looked and sounded convincing, but I wasn't ready to give up yet. "Well, as I said, I think most people are assuming *you're* behind it, Mr. Ayers—that it's all just part of the fun."

He shook his head vigorously. "But I don't know anything about it!" He sighed and tugged at his white suit jacket. "I just don't know what to make of it all, Nancy. I have no idea how those things keep happening. Unless . . ."

"Unless what?"

He peered at me, and then turned to stare into the fireplace. "Oh, I'm sure you'll think I'm just a silly old man. Living in this house alone for so many years, you sometimes see things. . . . I suppose I've grown accustomed to living with Grandmother Lisette. I didn't think she'd have any reason to try to interfere with this party. But then again, perhaps she disapproves of some of the improvements I've made to this place, or of selling off a few of her treasures." Suddenly his anxious expression lightened, and he winked at me. "Or perhaps she just doesn't like the party decorations."

I chuckled politely. "Perhaps. But you don't really believe this house is haunted, do you?"

"Of course I do!" Jackson seemed surprised by the question. "Surely you've heard the stories, Nancy."

I shrugged. "I figured they were just stories."

"You're a very intelligent young lady, Nancy Drew." He peered at me again, his eyes bright and focused. "I know you have a reputation for solving all sorts of puzzles and finding the solutions to difficult questions. But haven't you ever found a question you couldn't answer? Seen something you couldn't explain away with logic or clues?"

This conversation seemed to be taking a philosophical turn all of a sudden. Normally I wouldn't mind, but at the moment I didn't have the time. I was eager to move things back in a more useful direction.

"Sure," I joked. "I feel that way every time I turn on my laptop at home. As far as I'm concerned, computers must all be run by ghosts."

Jackson burst out laughing, seeming delighted. "Oh, my!" he exclaimed. "I certainly have to agree with you on that!"

I smiled at him. "So you aren't a computer person either?"

"Not at all," he assured me. "My niece Patricia and her husband got me one a couple of years ago to help me manage my finances and paperwork, but to this day I still can't work the dang thing!"

"Oh, dear!" I chuckled again sympathetically. "So you don't use it at all?"

Jackson shook his head with a sheepish smile. "Sometimes their daughter Maureen comes over and helps out—enters figures in the tax program and that sort of thing. She's a good girl," he said fondly, glancing across the room to where Maureen was dancing with her friends. "She does some other odd jobs for me as well— filing and such—for a bit of extra pocket money."

I hid my sudden flare of interest by taking a sip of my punch. "That's nice," I said, trying to think how I could find out more information. It sounded as if Maureen spent more time than I'd realized in this house—specifically at that computer where the notes had been composed and printed. And of course my friends and I had seen her in the office earlier. Could she be trying to frame Jackson, either with or without her mother's help? After all, if Jackson were accused of stealing back that tiara, he might have so many lawyers' fees to pay defending himself that he'd be forced to sell his most valuable asset—the house.

"Jackson! There you are." Mayor Simmons came striding toward us, trailed by her husband and daughter. "Oh hello, Nancy. Sorry to interrupt. But we have to be going, and I wanted to be sure to thank our host for the lovely evening."

"No problem, Mayor Simmons," I said. "I was just about to excuse myself to get another drink anyway. See you all later."

I hurried off. Seeing that people were starting to leave made me more anxious than ever to get this case solved, but before I could find my friends, Deirdre buttonholed me near the catering table.

"Did you find it yet?" she demanded.

"Not yet," I said, holding up my hands, which held nothing but my mask and purse. "But don't worry, we're getting closer," I said quickly. "I'm looking into a new suspect right now."

"Really? Who?" she demanded, grabbing my arm and digging her fingers into my skin.

"Ow!" I yanked my arm away. "Maureen Ardmore. It sounds like she might have reason to want to spook her great-uncle. She couldn't have been the one who actually grabbed the tiara, but if she was working with—hey! Where are you going?"

Deirdre had just spun on her heels and marched away. My eyes widened when I realized she was heading straight toward Maureen and her friends across the room.

I raced after Deirdre and grabbed her. "Stop," I ordered. "Don't do anything stupid."

"You just said you think Maureen did it, right?" Deirdre was glaring at Maureen, though Maureen was still too far away to notice. "I'm going to tell her where she can stick her stupid ransom demands." She gritted her teeth. "I always knew that girl was strange, but I never thought—"

"Wait, you can't do that." I didn't loosen my grip on her arm. "We don't have any proof yet. If you accuse her and she's guilty, it gives her a chance to cover her tracks. And if you accuse her and she's *not* guilty—"

Deirdre finally tore her gaze away from Maureen and glared at me instead. "I thought you just said she did it!"

"I said she's a *suspect*," I corrected. Just then I spotted Adam making his way through the crowd toward us. I smiled, suddenly incredibly glad to see him— and, for once, glad that Deirdre had let him in on the secret. "Adam!" I called out.

He hurried over. "What's up?" he asked with a worried glance at Deirdre.

"You need to keep an eye on her," I told him

bluntly. "I'm getting closer to some answers, and she wants to rush around accusing people before we can prove anything. Talk some sense into her, okay?"

Deirdre rolled her eyes. "I'm standing right here, you know, Nancy."

Ignoring her, I gave Adam a warning look. "I'm counting on you," I told him. Then I turned and hurried off.

I didn't see my friends anywhere in the main room. Figuring they might be out by the stairwell, I headed that way. But halfway to the arched doorway I passed Mr. Fielding, who was standing alone gazing at a small antique inkwell on an end table. Deciding I might as well take a moment to question him, I veered over. Even if he and Adam weren't in on the theft together, it was possible that Mr. Fielding was working with someone else. He still had one of the best motives of anyone present, other than Jackson and his relatives.

"Hello again, Mr. Fielding," I greeted him. "Having a nice time?"

He looked up and blinked at me. "Hello, Nancy," he said, adjusting the pocket watch resting on his ample stomach. "Yes, just fine. And you?"

"Great." I smiled. "I've especially been enjoying the little ghostly touches this evening. Very atmospheric, don't you think?"

He frowned. "I'm afraid I can't agree with you there, young lady," he said, his voice disapproving. "Very foolish, all that business. I wouldn't have thought Jackson the type, really." His frown deepened. "Of course, I also wouldn't have thought that Shannon girl would take off the Ayers tiara after she forced my son to beg me to let her wear it tonight."

"So you noticed that Deirdre took the tiara off," I commented. I glanced over toward where I'd last seen Deirdre and Adam, but they were nowhere in sight. I could only hope she hadn't rushed off to accuse anyone.

Mr. Fielding let out a little snort. "Of course I noticed," he grumbled. "From what I understand, she shoved it into her handbag because it was messing up her hair or some such foolishness."

"Yes, that's too bad," I said. "Having her wear it would have been nice publicity for Olde River Jewelers."

"Well, yes, of course there's that." He smiled at me. "I can see you have a head for business, Nancy, just like your father." He clutched his pocket watch as his smile faded. "But it's also a bit of an insult to me, isn't it? After I was generous enough to loan it to her . . ." He shook his head and gave another little snort of disapproval. "Then again, I don't know why I should have expected otherwise, really. I'm almost starting to think Adam's mother and I should send Adam on that London trip after all—at least that way he'd be away from her for a while."

The last couple of sentences were half under his breath, and I wasn't sure he'd even meant for me to hear them. But recalling what Adam had mentioned earlier about his planned trip to London that summer, I couldn't help being curious.

"Did you say something about Adam going to London?" I asked innocently.

"Well, he *wants* to go gallivanting off with a group of hooligans from his fraternity house." He pursed his fleshy lips. "His mother and I said no, of course. I'm not about to let a son of mine goof off in another country when he could be here at home getting some solid business experience at the store. Why, I haven't even met these fraternity brothers that he plans to go with! Quite childish, really. I'm sure your father would agree. Speaking of which, it's really a shame Carson couldn't make it tonight."

"Yes, I know Dad is sorry to have missed it," I said. "Well, if you'll excuse me, I—"

"I was very impressed to hear about the way he handled the Union Street zoning lawsuit last month," Mr. Fielding went on, not seeming to have heard me. "It takes a very talented attorney to sort out something like that without making either side angry, but it figures Carson could do it if anyone could. . . ."

For several excruciatingly long minutes, I stood there and listened to Mr. Fielding chatter on about what a great guy my dad is. Sometimes it's not a good thing to have such a universally admirable father.

Finally I managed to interrupt long enough to make an excuse and escape. I hurried off toward the stairwell.

Sure enough, Bess, George, and Ned were there waiting for me. They all looked excited.

"Guess what, Nancy?" George exclaimed as I skidded to a stop in front of them. "We just solved the case!"

12

A Surprising Confession

Huh?" I said, surprised. "What do you mean, you solved it?"

"We found another clue." Bess nudged Ned. "Show her."

Ned pulled a piece of paper out of his jacket pocket and handed it to me. "We took a quick look upstairs, but we didn't see much up there. So we came back down and did a little more snooping around in the computer room," he explained. "George found this on top of a little pile of papers on the desk. See? It's a printout of tonight's guest list."

I saw that he was right. There were some notes and markings scribbled in the margins of the list. Bess pointed at a couple of them.

"Check it out," she said. "There's a big X right by Deirdre's name. And look what's written near it!"

"'L's tiara,'" I read aloud. "Interesting. We should check out the handwriting and see—"

"Already done," George interrupted smugly. "It's Maureen's. She always dots her i's with little slashes like that."

"We checked it against a bunch of other stuff in the office," Bess explained. "There are lots of notes and things she wrote to Jackson in there."

"Oh, right," I said. "Jackson told me she does a lot of computer work for him."

"We know," Ned said, resting one arm on the banister. "Deirdre and Adam told us. They said they'd just talked to you."

"Oh." I could tell my friends were expecting me to be as excited as they were. And I couldn't blame them. They were sure they'd solved the case. I had to admit, those margin scribbles were pretty incriminating. But somehow I wasn't quite convinced.

"What?" George demanded, peering at me. "Why do you have that weird look on your face?"

"I know that look," Bess said. "It's Nancy's patented *I have a hunch* look."

"You're right," I admitted. "And this time I have a hunch that the solution can't be this easy."

Ned looked a bit crestfallen. "What do you mean?" he asked. He took the piece of paper from my hand and glanced at it.

"What more do you want?" George added. "A photo on my camera of Maureen dancing around wearing that tiara and going, 'Na-na-na, I stole this'?"

"Don't forget, Maureen has a solid alibi for the time of the theft," I reminded them. "Half the room remembered seeing her dancing."

Bess nodded. "But we already talked about how she might have an accomplice," she said. "Jackson, or her mother . . ."

"Or how about that guy Steve she was hanging out with earlier?" George suggested, kicking absently at the foot of the staircase. "He was sort of a trouble-maker in high school, wasn't he?"

"He wasn't that bad. But he wasn't exactly an alter boy, either," Ned said. "I could go find an excuse to talk to him if you want."

"Good idea." George looked excited again. "And the rest of us could talk to Patricia. All we have to do is figure out which one has been working with Maureen, and voila! Even Miss Skeptical here will be convinced." She waved a hand at me.

"What do you think, Nancy?" Bess looked at me. "It all makes sense, right? After all, what seems impossible for

114

one person is no problem for two working together—alibi or no alibi."

I didn't answer for a second. Something about what she'd just said was setting off my hunch-o-meter. But I wasn't sure why.

"Nancy?" George prompted after a moment of silence. "Earth to Nancy!"

I blinked at her. "Hey, George, what happened after that crash when the lamp fell?" I asked. "I mean *exactly*."

George looked surprised by the sudden change of topic. So did the others.

"I ran up the stairs here." George gestured to the staircase rising up behind us. "When I got up to the second-floor hallway, I saw the tipped-over lamp right away. Then I heard a sort of click—it was a door being shut."

"Which direction did the noise come from?" I asked.

"That way." She pointed toward the left side of the house. "Anyway, I went over and opened the door I thought it was. It led to this little room in the corner right next door to Lisette's bedroom. I saw Derek through the window. He was standing on the balcony on the side of the house."

I turned and headed down the hall. My mind was still turning over what I knew about the case so far.

"Where are you going?" Bess asked.

"Come outside for a sec," I said. "I just want to check on something."

I hurried to the side door and stepped outside. Glancing to the left, I saw the side porch, which opened directly into the main party area. Then I looked at the right and saw the fire-escape-style staircase rising up to the second floor.

"Is that the balcony where you saw Derek?" I asked, pointing up to the landing of the fire escape.

George nodded. "That's the one," she said. "Why? You don't still think he had something to do with this, do you? I'll admit the guy seems shady. But he couldn't have stolen the tiara. He was with Bess the whole time it was happening, remember?"

Bess wrinkled her forehead. "Are you thinking he could be Maureen's accomplice, Nancy?"

"That would sort of make sense, since we did see them talking together," Ned said. "But they're also the only two people we know of with solid alibis during the theft."

I rubbed my chin and stared up at the balcony. "If Maureen was clever enough to concoct—or even *help* concoct—this whole plan," I said, thinking aloud, "then how would she be stupid enough to leave that incriminating list just lying around where anyone could find it? It doesn't make sense."

"I guess." Bess sounded uncertain. "But are you

saying someone was trying to frame her? That seems awfully random."

"I know." I chewed on my lower lip. "And I won't deny that Maureen makes a pretty good suspect in some ways—almost better than Derek. But how would he even know about the tiara in the first place?"

"Hmm, good point," George said. "So what do we do now?"

I sighed and glanced around at the three of them. "I don't know," I admitted. "I just have a nagging feeling we're missing something here."

"Can we look for it inside?" Bess rubbed her arms. "It's chilly out here."

We headed back in. "Let's go over everything we know so far," I suggested. "Maybe if we talk through it, something will—"

Deirdre's screech cut me off. "Where have you been? I've been looking all over for you!"

She didn't look good. Her eyes were frantic, her face was pale with bright red spots on her cheeks, and even her carefully coiffed hair was starting to come loose. I wondered if she'd escaped from Adam—he was nowhere in sight.

"Relax, Deirdre," I said. "We're working on—"

She didn't let me finish. "Stop telling me to relax!" she shrieked, throwing both hands in the air. "The party will be over in like twenty minutes! We're running out of time!"

She raced off before any of us could make a move to stop her. "Uh-oh," Ned said. "She looks a little unhinged."

"I hope she doesn't do anything stupid," I said grimly. But I couldn't worry about that at the moment. As Deirdre herself had pointed out, we didn't have much time. "Okay, like I was saying, let's talk this over. We know that someone ambushed Deirdre in the bathroom and took the tiara. Ten or fifteen minutes later, the lights all went out and that music played."

"Do you think those things are definitely connected?" Bess asked.

"I'm really starting to," I said. "My little talk with Jackson convinced me that he's not behind any of the 'ghostly' happenings tonight. So I'm thinking someone has been staging them as a distraction."

"Distraction?" Ned repeated. "For what?"

I shrugged. "Maybe to spook Deirdre," I said. "Or maybe to throw us off the trail if the thief knew that Deirdre had told us about the stolen tiara. Causing a lot of confusion would work either way."

"Makes sense, I suppose," George said.

We had wandered across the stairwell area and down the kitchen hallway toward the solarium as we talked. Now Bess stopped and stared into the darkened solarium.

"So you think someone staged that blackout, and the weird lights in the solarium . . ." She ticked the occurrences off on her fingers.

"And the mask in the punch bowl," Ned added. "And that weird figure in the window from George's photos."

I rested a hand on the solarium window, staring inside. "We need to figure out how all those things were done, and that might tell us who could have done them," I mused aloud. "Which suspect—or combination of suspects—had the opportunity and knowledge to pull this off?"

"Right," Ned agreed. "Let's take Patricia and Maureen first. They both had the knowledge of the tiara, and of this house. Maureen couldn't have done the theft because several people saw her dancing while the theft was taking place, but was she around during the blackout?"

We talked through all the angles. Only Maureen and Derek had alibis for the theft. Jackson definitely had been in the main room during the blackout, as had Adam, but none of us were entirely sure about anyone else. The mask in the punch bowl could have been done most easily by Jackson, who had been nearby, and least easily by Maureen, who had been lounging in the office just a few minutes later. Then again, just about anyone else probably could have dropped that mask in the punch without much trouble. Then there was the figure in the window—that was a tricky one too.

We went through every suspect and likely combination of suspects we could imagine—Patricia and Maureen, Maureen and Jackson, Patricia and Jackson, Derek and Maureen, Adam and his father, Mr. Fielding and Derek, Jackson and Derek, Patricia and Derek. Somehow, though, none of them quite seemed to work.

"The problem is that figure in the window," I said, glancing over at George with a troubled frown. "During the time that you were off snapping that photo, I'm pretty sure *all* of our suspects were visible at the party. I remember seeing Jackson, Maureen, and Patricia all standing together, because I was on my way over to try to question them. But then I got stopped by Deirdre and Adam, and I'm pretty sure Adam's father was around too. And Derek was there, because he spotted Deirdre after a minute and started coming toward us."

Bess shook her head. "I know," she said. "There's no way any of them could have placed that figure, then gone back and removed it before George got upstairs. I'm starting to wonder if there's a suspect under our noses that we've totally missed."

"Can I see that photo again, George?" I asked. "*I'm* starting to wonder if maybe that ghost photo might have a more innocuous explanation—maybe a lost or curious party guest wandering around upstairs rather than another ghost event."

Ned chuckled. "Or maybe it's a *real* ghost, and George is about to strike it rich just like she hoped."

George handed over the camera. I noticed her face was kind of red, but I didn't think much of it. If she was annoyed by Ned's joke, I didn't have time for it right now.

"Okay, let's see," I murmured, scrolling quickly through the photos on the camera's memory. "Here it is. . . ."

"Wait!" George blurted out. "Don't bother trying to analyze it, Nancy. *I'm* the one who faked that picture, okay? It was me!"

13

Photo Finish

What?" **Bess exclaimed. She** grabbed the camera from me and looked at the viewer. "*You* faked this, George? Why?"

George kicked at the floor, her expression wavering between defiance and guilt. "When I realized I wasn't going to get anything real that was good enough for TV, I started to experiment a little," she said. "First I tried that foggy-mirror shot. But that didn't seem to impress anyone too much. So I got the idea to set up the camera on the porch rail on a timer, then run up the outside steps and pose in the corner window."

"Gee, no wonder you didn't find anything when you ran back up there afterward," Bess said sarcastically.

George shrugged. "I know. I just went up to hide the pillowcase I had over my head for the picture so

122

nobody would find it and figure it out." She glanced at me. "You can't be too careful with a detective in the house."

I took the camera back to look again at the photos. Clicking through the set of "ghost in the window" pictures, I couldn't help admiring George's technique. She'd really made her shot look spooky. But there was no time to compliment her on that—or lecture her about the ethics of faking a ghost, for that matter. All that would have to wait.

"Okay, this changes things a bit," I said, still scrolling slowly through the photos on the camera. I hadn't realized quite how many photos she'd taken that evening—there were not only a number of shots of Lisette's bedroom, the solarium, and other parts of the house, but also quite a few crowd scenes from the party itself. "But it still doesn't give us any real answers."

"I know," Ned said with a sigh. "We need to figure this out. Who had the motive?"

"Just about anyone," Bess pointed out. "That tiara is valuable—both sentimentally and otherwise."

"Right. The more important issue is who had the opportunity." I continued scrolling absently through the photos, thinking hard about all our suspects. "Could Derek have been working with an outside partner who sneaked in and out again, like Adam suggested earlier, or . . . ?"

My voice trailed off as I stared at the photo that had just come up. George leaned closer.

"What?" she said. "What are you looking at?"

"When did you take this one?" I held it up. The photo was another crowd shot, but at one side Adam and Derek were clearly visible in the background leaning toward each other.

George squinted at it. "I don't know," she said. "It should say on the readout. Why? Isn't that just those two jerks fighting over Deirdre again?"

"It does look that way, at least at first glance," I said. "But where's Deirdre?"

Bess and Ned were both gathered around by now as well. "Hey, they're not even in the main room," Bess said. "That looks like the kitchen."

"And neither of them look angry for once," Ned added.

I stared at the photo. The two guys were indeed in the kitchen, surrounded by busy-looking caterers. They appeared to be having a conversation.

"I guess I didn't even notice them when I took that shot," George said. "But check it out—there they are, clear as day. Pretty awesome camera, huh?"

I smiled. "Really awesome camera. It just solved the mystery!"

14

A Ghostly Good-Bye

All my friends started talking at once. But there was no time to tell them more than the bare minimum of what I'd just figured out. I didn't want to take the chance that Deirdre would give up and just ask her parents for the money.

"I'll be back soon," I told my friends. "And I promise, I'll explain everything then."

I ran off before they could protest. All the pieces had finally clicked into place. Why hadn't I seen it before?

Mr. Fielding was over near the punch bowl. Luckily Chief McGinnis was still at the party too. Soon I'd told them both the whole story.

"Are you sure about this, Nancy?" The chief sounded a bit dubious. For some reason, he's not always impressed by my amateur detective work. "You're making a very serious accusation here."

But Mr. Fielding looked grim. "We'd better look into this, McGinnis," he said. "I have a feeling I might know what it's all about." He stared across the room.

Following his gaze, I saw Deirdre and Adam dancing. Derek was lounging around nearby, trading dirty looks with Adam. When the three of us approached them, I think Adam knew right away that the jig was up. His face sort of crumpled.

"Um, what's up?" he asked.

"We just have a few questions we'd like you to answer," the chief began. He pointed at Derek, who was in the process of slinking away. "You too, young man."

But I guess Mr. Fielding wasn't in the mood to waste time following police procedure. "Where is it?" he demanded bluntly, glowering at his son.

"Where's what?" Adam asked weakly.

"That tiara." Mr. Fielding crossed his arms over his chest. "Don't bother lying to me, Adam. Miss Drew explained it all."

Deirdre looked perplexed. "What's going on?" She let out a gasp, and then glared at me furiously. "You'd better not have told them what I told you!"

"I'm sorry, Miss Shannon." Mr. Fielding was still frowning at Adam, who was staring at the floor. "It appears my son and his friend have used you for their own disgraceful purposes."

"Huh?" Deirdre wrinkled her nose, shooting a confused look at Derek. "What are you talking about? Adam isn't friends with that guy. Actually the two of them have been fighting over me all night." She patted her hair, allowing a self-satisfied smirk to come over her face.

"Not quite, Deirdre," I spoke up. "Actually, they've been *pretending* to fight over you to make it look like they're strangers who hated each other on sight. That way nobody would ever suspect them of being in cahoots. But this whole time they've really been working together to extort that ransom money out of you."

"*What?*" Deirdre shrieked. She spun around to face Adam. "No way. That's not true, is it? *Is it?* Answer me!"

Adam's gaze flicked from her to his father and back again. I couldn't help feeling a little bit sorry for him. He probably wasn't sure who to be more scared of.

"You should probably just tell us the truth, Adam," I said gently. "It will be easier for everyone that way."

"Don't say anything!" Derek spoke up for the first time, sounding a bit hysterical. "Dude, they can't make us say a word without a lawyer present!"

Adam sighed, suddenly looking defeated. "No,

Nancy's right," he said. "Come on—I'll show you where we hid the tiara."

A few minutes later it was all over—both the party and the case. I found my friends lounging on the leather couches in the office.

"Well?" Ned asked, sitting up straight as I walked in.

"Were you right?" Bess added. "Were Adam and Derek working together?"

"Uh-huh." I dropped my mask and purse on a chair and perched on the arm. "Adam cracked almost as soon as his father and Chief McGinnis started questioning him. Derek was a little more stubborn, but he finally confessed too."

George shook her head. "I still can't believe it," she declared. "I was sure those two hated each other!"

Ned nodded. "If Nancy hadn't noticed them together in George's photo and put two and two together . . ."

"They'd planned never to be seen together unless they were fighting over Deirdre to keep up the charade," I said. "I guess when Deirdre came to me for help, they sort of panicked and had that quick meeting in the kitchen."

"Is that when they decided to start with the ghost stuff?" Ned asked.

I shrugged. "I guess so. Based on what I heard from Adam, it sounds like they'd planned the big blackout all along. That was meant to give Derek a chance to grab the tiara from where Adam had hidden it and get it out of the house. I think they also meant it to double as sort of a warning to Deirdre, just like we speculated—a way to remind her that they were in charge and she'd better not crack and tell anyone."

"Clever," George said. "But not clever enough to truly disable Deirdre's big mouth."

Bess giggled. "Okay, so wait," she said. "*Adam* was the one who actually mugged Deirdre in the bathroom?"

"Uh-huh," I said. "From what they said, it sounds like plan A was for Adam to get Deirdre outside on some pretense. Then he'd leave her there alone just long enough for Derek to pop out of the bushes behind her, grab the tiara, and give her the ransom note. But Adam couldn't get her out there, so they went with plan B."

"Talk about being prepared!" Ned commented.

I smiled. "I guess Adam warned Derek that Deirdre wasn't exactly . . . pliable, so they figured they'd have to be ready to improvise." I looked at George. "That's why you caught him snooping around upstairs early on—remember? When he broke that lamp?"

George nodded. "That's right! Except I didn't realize what he was doing at the time. But what about Adam?"

"Well, when Deirdre headed off to the bathroom

after that little scene on the dance floor, Adam pretended to get mad and stomp off outside. But actually he just went out on the side porch and immediately ducked back in through that other side door at the end of the office hallway. That way all he had to do was run up the hall, turn off the light outside the bathroom, then go in and grab the tiara from Deirdre. He stashed it in a prearranged spot and then ducked back outside before Deirdre even got back to the main room."

"And that's when Derek hit the lights?" Ned asked.

I nodded. "When Adam was done hiding the tiara, all he had to do was give Derek some kind of signal that the deed was done, and Derek made the black-out happen."

"Wow." George looked impressed. "Adam must have been really nervous when he found out that Deirdre wanted to go to you for help."

"He tried to talk her out of it." I rolled my eyes. "But we all know how hard it is to change Deirdre's mind about anything. The best he could do was try to throw us off the trail after that. And lucky for him, he had easy access to all our theories and plans through Deirdre, which made it really simple to find ways to trip us up and distract us with random ghostliness."

Ned leaned forward. "So how do Adam and Derek

know each other, anyway? And why'd they do it? I mean, I don't know Derek at all, obviously. But Adam has never seemed like the law-breaking type."

"Well, I don't think I even mentioned it to you guys, because it didn't seem important at the time," I said. "But Adam told me earlier this evening that he was planning to spend this summer in London with some friends from college. Then later I heard from Mr. Fielding that he told Adam he couldn't go. He also mentioned that he didn't know some of the others who would be on the trip."

"Including Derek," George finished, her eyes lighting up as she made the connection.

"Exactly. Turns out they're fraternity brothers up in Chicago." I shrugged. "I guess they came up with this plan after Mr. Fielding said he wouldn't pay for the trip. Adam figured if he had his own funds, his dad couldn't say no."

Bess shook her head. "Knowing Mr. Fielding, I'm not sure that's true."

"I know what you mean," I said. "But I think Adam saw this whole plan as the solution to all his problems. Not only would it let him go on that trip, but he also thought it would impress Deirdre. See, he'd planned to volunteer to go to the 'bad guy' with the ransom money at the end of the party, supposedly to spare Deirdre from the danger."

"I get it," Bess said, nodding. "He thought he'd impress her so much with his dedication and bravery that she'd want to stay with him even if she'd been thinking of cutting him loose."

George snorted. "Bet Deirdre loved hearing all that. Her ego is going to be even more out of control than usual after this."

I smiled. "Maybe. But I think the writing was on the wall for that relationship anyway. She broke up with him as soon as she heard the whole story—though not before Mr. Fielding convinced her not to press charges."

"Probably helps that he's one of her dad's clients," Ned pointed out, leaning back in his seat again.

"Probably," I agreed. "He told her he wanted to take care of Adam's punishment himself, and that seemed to satisfy her. Anyway, Mr. Fielding got the tiara back—it was hidden under a bush in a neighbor's yard. Adam and Derek just wanted the money; they knew there was no way they could sell the thing without getting caught, not in a small town like River Heights. They confessed to all the ghostly hijinks, including the blackout, the mysterious music, the lights in the solarium, pushing me down outside . . ."

Bess's eyes widened. "I almost forgot about that, Nancy," she said. "They should be worried about *you* pressing charges—you could've been badly hurt!"

"It was Derek who shoved me," I said. "From what he said, it sounded like he was just planning to scare me. He even found some magnolia-scented spray up in Lisette's bedroom—I guess Jackson uses it for atmosphere during his historical tours. Derek seems to have a flair for the dramatic; apparently most of the ghost stuff was his idea. When I heard the little hiss of the spray bottle and started to turn around before he could get away, he panicked."

"So what's going to happen to Derek?" Ned asked.

"I'm not sure," I said. "I guess the police will have to figure that out. I'm just glad those two didn't manage to ruin Jackson's party or cause any serious damage."

"If anything, they probably helped," George said. "Most of the guests seemed to love all the ghost stuff."

I smiled. "I think you're right. I overheard Jackson talking to Mr. Fielding outside. It sounds like the fund-raiser was a huge success—lots of donations. Plus Mr. Fielding told him he wanted to make a pretty hefty donation himself to apologize for his son making so much trouble."

George grinned. "Tough luck for Patricia and Maureen, huh? Sounds like Jackson won't need to worry about selling the house now."

Just then we heard the sound of heavy footsteps

on the creaky floorboards out in the hall. Bess, who was closest to the door, leaned over and peeked out. "It's Mr. Fielding," she whispered.

A moment later Mr. Fielding passed the open door to the office. He spotted us and stopped short in the doorway.

"Oh, er, hello there," he said gruffly. "Miss Drew, could I possibly have a word with you?"

"Sure." I shot my friends a glance, stood up, and walked to the door. He turned and marched off a short distance before finally turning to face me.

He cleared his throat, looking a bit uncomfortable. "I'd like to thank you for turning up the truth this evening," he said in a stiff, formal voice. "I'm completely appalled by my son's behavior. And please trust me, he won't get off any easier with me than he would have with the police. Quite the contrary."

"You're welcome, Mr. Fielding." I wondered if Bess was right and he was about to beg me not to press charges regarding the shoving incident.

"Thanks to you, an important local heirloom is safe once again." Mr. Fielding locked his hands over his belly and glanced down at the tips of his shiny black shoes. "I never would have forgiven myself if it had disappeared for good. I hope you won't share this. . . ." He glanced at me, a hint of uncertainty in his eyes. "Well, I suppose I can trust you."

"What is it?" I asked, curious.

"There's a reason I keep that tiara in the vault instead of out on the display floor," he said. "I'm sure I could have sold it many times over if I'd advertised it. But I don't want to sell it—at least, not as long as Jackson Ayers is still alive." He glanced around the dark, old-fashioned hallway, once again looking slightly uncomfortable. "You see, that tiara belongs to this house," he went on. "I'd, er . . . well, I'd just hate to think of it going off somewhere else, unless perhaps it was back to New Orleans." He let his voice trail off, then cleared his throat again with a loud harrumph. "In any case," he said, his voice once again formal and stiff. "Thank you, Nancy. We all appreciate what you've done tonight."

"You're very welcome," I said, a little stunned by what I'd just heard.

Who'd have thunk it? I thought as I watched him hurry off toward the front of the house. It seems even dour old Mr. Fielding has a bit of a sentimental side! Guess that just goes to prove the old adage about not judging a book by its cover.

I'd been reminded of that in more than one way that night, I realized, turning to wander slowly back to my friends. We'd all spent most of the evening assuming that Adam and Derek were strangers who had suddenly become mortal enemies. Their masks and costumes hadn't thrown us off nearly as much as

135

their behavior, and that had almost let them get away with the crime.

When I got back to the office, I told the others what Mr. Fielding had said. They were just as surprised as I had been to discover the existence of the jeweler's warmer, fuzzier side.

"I know how he feels, though," Bess said as we all picked up our things and got ready to leave. "It would just be wrong somehow to think of Lisette's tiara in a stranger's hands. It's bad enough it's in the vault at Olde River Jewelers and not right here in this house where it belongs."

"I know," I said. "But if Lisette really *were* haunting this place . . ." I shot a glance at George, remembering her earlier mission. "Well, I bet she really would understand why Jackson had to sell it."

Bess nodded. "If she *is* around, I bet she enjoyed tonight's party, too," she said. "It probably reminded her of home—maybe brought some New Orleans–style fun back into her lonely ghostly existence."

"Come on," Ned said through an amused smile. "It's getting late. We should clear out and let Jackson have his house back."

Soon we were walking through the stairwell area on our way toward the front room. "Hold on a second," I said. "I want to use the bathroom before we head out."

There was a framed Mardi Gras fan and mask

hanging in the bathroom that I hadn't noticed before. Seeing them made my mind wander back to Lisette. Just being in her old house and chasing down her missing tiara had made me feel closer to her somehow. I could almost imagine her drifting through that old solarium, sniffing the long-lost scent of magnolias and smiling over what we'd done. . . .

I shook my head and chuckled at myself. It wasn't like me to be so fanciful.

It must be that wild Mardi Gras atmosphere, I thought as I got ready to wash my hands. It can make you start to believe in just about anything, I guess.

Suddenly the lights flickered overhead. I glanced up with a frown, wondering if George was messing with me. I was about to call out to my friends, but before I could do so a soft riff of music surrounded me, jazzy and sprightly and joyful-sounding.

For a moment I froze in panic. What if Derek and Adam hadn't been the only ones in on tonight's crime? What if there was another accomplice, and he had tracked me down here and distracted my friends somehow, planning to burst in and grab me just as they'd done to Deirdre?

Before I could finish the thought, the music was gone and the lights were back to normal. I blinked, suddenly unsure that it had even happened. It was getting pretty late, and I was tired.

Still, as I reached for the door, I cast one last glance at the framed Mardi Gras mask and fan, their spirited colors and bright beads muted by the dusty glass. Suddenly I remembered that burst of sad-sounding jazz music I'd thought I'd heard on the way into the party—well before that knock on the head.

Outside I found Ned leaning against the wall beside the door. "Bess and George went on ahead," he said.

"You were standing outside the door the whole time, right?" I asked him.

He nodded. "Of course. Are you okay? You look a little spooked."

I could tell he was telling the truth. "Did you—um—notice anything weird?"

He looked a little confused. "Weird?" he repeated.

I shrugged my shoulders and looked around one last time. Nothing seemed out of the ordinary anymore.

Ned took my hand and we started walking away. We'd just made it to the main room. Seeing that George had stopped to fiddle with her camera, I opened my mouth to say something. But then I closed it again.

Maybe there are some mysteries that are better left unsolved.